THE SAND PONIES

THE
SAND PONIES

SHIRLEY ROUSSEAU MURPHY

Illustrated by Erika Weihs

THE VIKING PRESS   NEW YORK

For J.L. and for Helen and Mabel

CHAPTER

1

A young girl sleeps in a small, drab room. In her dream she watches the surf beat against a rocky cliff, filling the tide pools and casting spray to the meadows above.

Far away a small buckskin horse lifts his head and listens in vain for the pounding of the sea.

The room is still and very dim. There is only one window, facing a light well, a brick-lined shaft down which little of the dawn can come. The noise and shouting in the apartment have subsided and the bedroom door is locked from inside.

The room has not cooled off during the night, but still holds the stale heat of yesterday, and the two children sleep with only sheets over them, the boy tossing fitfully. They are children too old to be shar-

ing a room, but share they must, for there is no other, except their aunt and uncle's, and a small ugly sitting room and a kitchen like the inside of a brown box. The whole apartment is like this, the wallpaper used and dirty looking, the ceiling paint colorless with grime, the windows small and unwashed, the carpets and furniture unpleasant to sit on and touch.

In Karen's dream the sun is bright. She is sitting astride the buckskin horse, watching the pasture grass blow and listening to the crash of the surf. The horse tosses his head, and in her sleep Karen smiles a little and her lashes move softly on her freckled cheeks.

She is well freckled. Both children are. Like flecks of gold the freckles spatter their noses and cheeks, the only brightness in the room. She is older than Tom by a year, but he is taller. They are twelve and thirteen.

"I could pass for sixteen. So could you. We're tall enough. We could get jobs," was the last thing she had said before she went to sleep, the door bolted against the drunken shouting of their uncle.

Yes, we're tall enough, Tom had thought. Maybe we could. He had reached to check the lock on the door, then fallen asleep himself almost at once.

It had started early the previous morning, with Uncle George pouring whisky into his coffee. The children had gulped their breakfasts and got out into the street, but at noon hunger had forced them back again. "It'll be awful," Karen had said. It was. They could hear their uncle and aunt shouting before they got near the door, and as the children slipped down the hall to the kitchen the dim apartment was nearly unbearable with the smell of whisky.

There was more shouting as they hurriedly gathered together peanut butter and bread, milk and glasses, and a knife.

"You shouldn't hear words like that," Tom said.

"And what about you?"

"But you're a girl."

"Doesn't matter," Karen said. "Come on."

As they ate, staring out the dirty window at the

brick wall, trying to ignore the shouting, they talked, as they had so many times, about what to do.

There were only three things. The first was to run away, and this was the most attractive. Now that school was out their need was greater than ever; and it would be easier.

The second thing was the most sensible. "But what would they do with us if we did go to the authorities?" Karen said. They were afraid to find out.

The third thing, of course, was to stay where they were and make the best of it until they were old enough to leave. Eighteen was forever. "Like trapped animals," Karen said.

The delight of running away haunted them. Summer lay outside the city, summer and fields and freedom. But they weren't stupid children. There was everything against its working.

"They would find us," Karen said.

"Maybe not," Tom answered.

And if they were found, what then? Who would find them? Not Aunt and Uncle, surely; they wouldn't care. Then it would be the authorities. Would they put them in a home for orphans? Separate them? Or would the children be put up for adoption, each going to a different family? "A different city, likely," Karen said. "They might make it worse for us, worse than if we went to them right off."

Tom thought it wouldn't make any difference. "They'd see we couldn't stay here. Someone would understand." Tom had more faith in people than Karen did. Karen had little faith in anyone any more, except Tom and herself.

It had been harder for her than for him. She is a girl, and softer, Tom thought, though he knew that she could stand some things better than he. Still, the last year had been harder on her. She seemed to draw strength from the country and the sea, and had needed these things, and her pony, badly those first weeks after their parents had been killed so suddenly. When the children had been moved to the city she had grown pale and listless.

After the funeral the children had hoped they could stay on the farm; no one would know, or care. But this was not the case. Somehow, what they thought right didn't seem right to anyone else. The farm had been sold, and worse, so had the four horses, who were all that was left from their life with Mother and Dad, all that was left of their childhood, it seemed.

Karen missed Kippy so badly that sometimes at night she thought she could put out her hand and feel his soft gold neck and his tangled black mane. No one would tell the children where the horses were, and Karen still cried for them, in a way quite different from the way that she cried for Mother and Dad. Their parents were dead, and there was a huge empty spot in the middle of Karen that would never go away; but she knew she would see them again at the end of everything, a long way off. It was like looking down a dim tunnel to something brilliant at the other end.

She cried for the horses because they could be hungry, hurt, all the things living creatures can be. She thought that she and Tom were the only ones who would help them, who would care.

In her dream she rides Kippy, galloping, along the cliff above the sea, the wind blowing salty spray in her face, Mother following on her chestnut mare, then Tom and Dad, Dad's big bay bucking a little and Tom's mare, Tolly, shying at rabbits.

Karen is smiling as she wakes, but instead of sunshine, here is the dismal room, and the empty hurt to engulf her once more. The picture on the dresser is all that is left of that life—the big house standing comfortably between the willows, facing the sea, the family mounted, the horses looking eager.

Karen closes her eyes and curls tight under the covers. She wishes she would die, but she knows you do not die of unhappiness, and she thinks back to the day of the funeral. It was a cold, blustery day, and there seemed to be a great deal of black—the hearse, the strange pallbearers; somehow all the flowers meant nothing. She was glad it was cold, that the wind blew. Even the pastor's face did not seem real. He talked to her for a long time after the funeral, when Tom had gone off by himself. She did not listen to him at first, but as he talked she began to listen. "There are things you must do for your parents now, Karen," the pastor repeated. Karen did listen to this. "You are the measure of their lives now," he continued. "If you were to give up living you would kill something belonging to them. What you do with your life, Karen, will be the proof of their worth as well as your own." He paused, looking at her. "Will you disappoint them?"

She knew she would not. Nor would Tom.

She dozes again, and when she wakes the room is lighter and the uncle's yelling has started once more. The language is vile. Tom is awake, too, sitting by the window spreading peanut butter on a slice of bread. He hands it to her and spreads another. The musty smell of the room makes the peanut butter taste stale, but it fills a little bit of Karen's empty stomach, and after three slices of bread she gets up to wash and dress. She hates going out into the hall, and makes Tom lock the door behind her and wait for her soft knock.

"It's never been this bad before," Tom says as they sit staring dismally out the window, listening. There is a loud crash, and Aunt Hester yells incoherently. The pattern is always the same. There seems to be no night or day for the uncle and aunt when they are drinking, no pattern to the days save their own drunken one. As the drinking starts there is gross laughter, ribald joking. This grows louder until anger creeps into the voices. Then there is fighting, followed by crying, or sometimes a slam as one or the other goes out, only to return later and begin again. There are pauses for sleeping, sometimes for eating, and the children tiptoe around the house and stay out of it as much as they can.

Sometimes the children are drawn in against their will, and taunted. This is the worst of all. They have learned to keep their door locked.

There is another loud crash, and Aunt Hester screams.

"What if he kills her?" Karen whispers, terrified.

"If he kills her," Tom says, "there will be the authorities, for sure. We'd better make up our minds, Karen. We can't stay any longer. Which will it be?"

Karen looks at Tom for a long time; then she opens the closet door and begins to stuff things into a canvas knapsack. Tom squeezes in beside her, gives her a hug, and begins to do the same, taking a little packet of money from his boot and dividing the contents between them. There isn't much. "How far will it get us?" Karen asks.

"On a bus, a good way," Tom says. "Forty-two eighty in all." There is a sudden silence outside. The children hurry faster.

They wait for the noise to begin again to shield their trip down the hall to the front door. Finally, drunken shouting comes from the kitchen. Out they creep, Tom leading.

"Wait," Tom whispers. "The note." He pins it to

the curtain of the front door. Someone going out might read it, while elsewhere in the house it could go unnoticed. It is a sensible note; they are resourceful children. It could very well mean their freedom in the days to come.

Dear Aunt Hester and Uncle George,

We do not want to stay any longer, and we think you will not care if we go away. We will provide for ourselves.

If no one knows we are gone you will be able to go on receiving the money Mother and Dad left in trust. You know that if we are not happy here we can be made Wards of the Court, and the trust will be changed. If you can make it seem that we are still living here, we will all be better off.

We do not hold any grudge, but just want to live our own lives in our own way.

Tom and Karen

The children hurry down the two flights of stairs, skirting trash boxes, and out into the alley, then along the early-morning streets until they reach the bus station, where the first commuters are beginning to make a bustle of activity.

The children share a cup of cocoa from a machine and look at the schedules. There is only one way to go, and that is north. Something nearly as strong as life itself draws them, though they know they cannot go home. "How far is it?" Karen asks as they board the bus.

"How far is what?" Tom says, knowing very well what she means.

"How far . . . well, how far until we'll be safe in the country?" she whispers.

As the bus creeps through the center of the metropolitan area the day has begun to warm and the traffic is growing thicker.

"I think about five hundred miles," Tom says as they get settled. He looks steadily at Karen. "It is eleven hundred miles to home, Karen. We can't go there. We'd be found." They are sitting quite alone at the back of the bus.

"I know," Karen says. "I forgot for a minute."

He puts his arm around her. They are handsome children, but they look very sad. Sadness lies just below the glow that adventure has given them, that freedom has given them.

By noon they are in the country, and they grow hungry as the smell of onions from the fields wafts through the bus windows. The farms seem green beyond belief after their long months in the city. There are crops of all kinds—lettuce, tomatoes, and the great fields of onions. When they stop for lunch they are famished and they eat two hamburgers each. "We can't do that often," Tom says, "or we won't get far. We must get jobs as soon as we can."

"I know," Karen says. "But weren't they good!" They board the bus again. "I think I can smell the ocean."

Tom grins at her, but soon, sure enough, they are passing between fields of fernlike artichoke, and beyond these they begin to catch glimpses of blue between the distant trees. "It is the ocean!" Karen says, and then, a minute later, "Look!"

Horses and riders are galloping along a path between the fields, and the children press their noses to the window longingly. "I wonder where Kippy is," Karen says sadly.

CHAPTER

2

The bus lurches and Karen wakes from dozing. They have crossed many miles of farm land and traveled for a while by the sea. Now they are coming into a stand of pines and redwood trees, towering up on both sides of the road. "Here?" Karen asks. "Could we live here?"

"Not yet," Tom says. It is a decision for both to make, but they are not yet far enough away. And they are still going north. If this country is lovely, home is lovelier; yet they know they can't go home.

At nightfall they reach San Francisco. They are tired and their courage is limp. "What if there is no night bus?" Karen asks. She is wild to get out of the city. "We can't afford a room, and no one would rent us one, anyway—they'd just report us. And if we stay in the station all night someone might notice." It is a wonder no one in the bus has asked why they are traveling alone. The back seat, and their extra height and mature looks have served them. But someone is to ask, later, and Tom is to answer, with an innocent, long-lashed smile, "Our grandmother is waiting for us. Mamma and Pappa put us on the bus this morning." No boy with such a smile could tell a lie.

There is a night bus, and it goes clear to Portland. "We could not stay on it that long," Tom says.

"I know," Karen answers, looking excited, "I know."

"Look," Tom says, crowding onto the edge of a bench and making room for Karen, "here is a local, going north along the coast, Karen. Two or three hours from now we could be in one of those little towns by the ocean. I think there are cattle ranches there."

"What kind of jobs could we get? Would a ranch hire us?"

"Sooner than city people, maybe."

"I could cook, if they needed a cook."

They have said these things before, but it is comforting to repeat them.

"It will be dark when we get off," Tom says. "No one will see us. We can sleep somewhere away from the town, and look around before we decide. We could be from San Francisco on a weekend."

"All right. Then if we don't like it we can go on tomorrow."

"Yes."

They find a cafeteria and buy a simple dinner, with extra sandwiches to go. Finally, fed and washed and feeling better, they settle down in the darkened bus and watch the city lights go by, the neon signs, the cars and apartments and street lights twinkling up the hills on both sides of them, then the lights of the bridge as they cross the mouth of the bay, and the scattered lights of the smaller towns, growing fewer until finally the bus is riding a high twisting road along the edge of a cliff. Far below is the ocean. They can see phosphorescence as the waves break white and glowing, and above them in the night there are stars, millions of stars. The only other light is the yellow path the bus makes before it along the mountain.

Soon they have passed through several villages. "We get off at the next one," Tom says. "I'd like to walk through town just like we lived there. I wonder if we dare?" Karen looks shocked. This is not Tom's way. "Maybe it's the night," he says. "Maybe it's being free. I just . . . well, I just want to walk around a little town at night. But perhaps we'd better not."

Karen smiles softly. "It'll be all right. I know it will. No one will pay any attention. Something hot would taste so good."

"Well, we'll see. Here we come." They are descending a steep hill, the bus's gears growling. Below are a few pale lights strung out in a row, a few splashes of colored neon, and some faint house lights farther on. Karen and Tom are the only ones to get off, walking softly past the sleeping passengers as the darkened bus stops at a corner. There is no station. A small shaggy dog greets them and follows them a way, but soon goes home to bed.

They start up the one street of the town, walking north. They pass a restaurant, a grocery and gas station, then farther on, another restaurant, small and grimy. In between the buildings stand pine and redwood trees, casting strange shadows in the glow from the street lights and shop signs, and overhead a sickle moon is rising beyond the hills. They walk slowly, breathing the salty air and feeling the space around them. They pass a feed store, a few more shops, and then an open space. The town is quite spread out, as if it didn't want to crowd in on itself. A good sign, Tom thinks. Then they come to an inn, set back a little from the road.

"I'd like to work there," Karen says, impressed. It is a neat place with deep balconies around the second floor. In the center is a patio in which a huge oak tree stands sheltering some deserted tables. There are lights in what appears to be the dining room; the children stop and yearn toward it. "Some cocoa would taste so good," Karen says.

Tom hesitates. "I guess there's no harm," he says finally, "if we hide our packs in the bushes. Maybe they'll have a job."

"What will we say if they do? That we live here?"

"No," Tom says. "I don't know." It's a dilemma they have not been able to solve. Then, "No. The town's too small. We don't know whether there are cabins or summer cottages where we *could* be living. We'd better have some cocoa and get the lay of the place, Karen, then wait until we've had a chance to look around some more, and make a plan."

"All right."

But when they have crossed the patio there is no restaurant, only a bar, and the occupants do not smile as the children enter. "What do you want?" asks the bartender. "Better go down to the Poppy, or Suzy's. This here's a bar, and kids not allowed."

"We're sorry," Tom says. "We didn't know. We just wanted coffee, that's all." They won't have cocoa in a bar.

"You got money, you'll get a cupa coffee," the man tells them gruffly, "but you gotta take it outside. There's tables in the patio." Everyone in the bar is staring, making the children uncomfortable. Tom quickly pays for the coffee and heads for the door, Karen beside him.

"You kids want a bed?" A gruff woman's voice stops them. She is a sinewy, tanned person with short dark hair. She is wearing a man's shirt and Levi's, and smoking a cigarette in a holder. She is sitting at a round wooden table with five men, poker chips and cards and glasses and ash trays scattered about. The men look equally sun-browned and rough, but somehow different from the cowboys and fishermen the children have known. Two have beards, and all have longish hair and mean-looking eyes.

"You kids want a bed?" she repeats.

"How could she have known? How could she?" Karen is to say later. Now they say nothing; both children are far too surprised. They just stand gaping.

"I could use a couple of dishwashers, and the floors need scrubbing." The woman continues, "You want a bed, you kids, or are you summer people?"

It is a chance for a job. Work and meals, and a room besides. Tom looks again at the bar and the rough men, and smells the stale beer smell. He looks at his sister, then gives the woman his best smile. "We hadn't thought about it. We really planned to loaf this summer. We'll ask our parents, though, if you need help. We won't want a room, of course. What will you pay, ma'am?"

"Ninety cents an hour, if you work good. Can you wait table, kid?" she asks Karen.

"I don't know why not," Karen says, poised.

"You ask your folks, kids," snaps the bartender. "Sixteen, ain'tcha? Must be. Don't want nothing ille-

gal going on around here." There is a snicker from
the poker table, and the woman glares for a second.

"We'll ask," Karen says, smiling. "We'll ask, and
come back in the morning. Thank you. And thanks,"
she says to the bartender, "for the coffee."

They drink their coffee at a table under the tree, looking at the stars through the branches and warming their hands around the steaming cups. They whisper a little, but dare not giggle over their deceitfulness. Karen's heart is pounding and she is glad when Tom returns their cups to the bar. "Well-brought-up kids," says the bartender. Several men chuckle.

"Just the thing for the Black Turtle," says one, and there is a murmur of laughter in the smoky room.

The children walk into the dusk of the road, retrieving their bags from the bushes.

"We'll not go back there," Tom says when they are out on the road once more. Most of the town is behind them, but there are a few tourist cabins with small Vacancy signs, and farther on, a blacksmith's shop.

"No," Karen says. She knows Tom is right, but the thought of waiting table interests her, and she is a little disappointed. "Maybe we only imagined there was anything strange about it. Maybe we are too touchy about bars and things, because of Uncle George."

Tom only looks at her.

"I guess it really wasn't a very nice place," she says reluctantly. Tom grins.

Now that the town is behind them the stars are brighter, and the moon sits like a golden scythe overhead. The ocean is louder, too, though they cannot see it, for the road is lined with scrubby, thick-growing trees.

A few cottages begin to appear, set back from the road, most of them dark, but here and there a light. "We would be best off sleeping near one of them,"

Tom says. "In case anyone bothered us, we could yell, or get to people for help."

There is a soft light ahead, and as they approach the cabin they see pale curtains and someone reading by the window. Close to the road is a giant willow tree, dropping its lacy branches to the ground. Tom parts the curtains of leaves, and there inside is a leaf-walled room, lighted faintly by the glow from the thin moon. They wait and listen. Nothing stirs, and the figure goes on reading. The children step inside and let the leaves fall together. They are completely hidden from the road and the house. They grin in the faint light and stealthily spread their tarpaulins out on the ground, taking care not to rustle the dry leaves. They settle down and pull their heavy coats over them. Karen is still thinking about the job.

"But we do need it badly," she whispers to Tom. "Couldn't we work for a little while, just to get some money, then go away? Before they find out we don't live here?" She doesn't dare whisper very loud, and Tom strains to hear.

"I'm afraid of it, Karen. I don't like that place."

She sighs.

"But maybe we'll feel differently in the morning."

"Yes, maybe," she says hopefully. "How would we work it? Would we take the room?"

"They'd know we lied to them."

"Would they care?"

"Not unless it were to their advantage, I think."

Karen knows he is right. "But couldn't we say that our folks are letting us do it for a lark? Or that they are going away for a couple of weeks, and will let us stay and work if we promise to do as we're told, and not go out anywhere at night after work? Something like that?"

"Perhaps," Tom says. "Let's see how it looks in the morning." They settle down to sleep, the sea singing to them and the willow tree rustling faintly overhead.

Much later the figure in the window puts out the light, then turns on another at the back of the house, preparing for bed. Finally this light, too, goes off, a window is opened, and then there is silence. In the distance a dog barks. Nearer, a wakeful bird twitters, and in the sky the moon climbs higher.

Karen does not stir to the cry of the bird or the little thud as the window is opened. She is dreaming, and in her dream she is standing beside an oilcloth-covered table in a brownish, dismal kitchen, and before her at the table sits her uncle, looking at her. His face is pale and lined, with red-rimmed eyes. He puts his hand on her shoulder and begins to shake her. Where is Tom to help her? She is terrified. The rank smell of whisky seems overwhelming. She looks around for Tom. He is not anywhere. She jerks away from the hand, the face laughing raucously at her, and she runs.

She is running through a dark tunnel, which echoes with her footsteps. Then a tiny light appears at the other end, and she is running toward it as fast as she can go, the sound of feet echoing in the tunnel behind her. She is breathless, winded; the light is growing no bigger. In a panic, she turns to face the one following her. She puts her hand to her mouth, but is unable to scream. Everything goes blurred; then suddenly a brilliant white light is all around her, and she is quite alone. Slowly the light turns to green and she is standing in a meadow, under a strange green sky. A little way off, looking at her, is Kippy. His legs are wet from the sea. She runs to him and puts her arms around his warm neck, but suddenly he is gone, and she is clutching her coat, and it is morning under the willow tree.

CHAPTER

3

The sun is pushing through the leafy walls of the willow, and a car is going along the road. From the nearby house comes the smell of frying bacon. Tom is dressed and sitting on his folded tarp, eating one of the last two sandwiches. He grins at Karen. His face is pink from scrubbing, and as she sits up and looks around she can see why. He has been in the yard of the house, found a bucket, and filled it with water. He has even brushed his teeth, for his wet toothbrush lies on top of his knapsack.

"How did you dare?" asks Karen, sniffing the cooking smell and peering between the leaves to see movements in what must be the kitchen window.

"I got it earlier, when it was still pretty dark. We should put it back, but I don't think we'd better, now. Hurry up. When he sits down to eat might be the best time to leave." They can smell coffee, too, and hear the clatter of dishes.

Karen hurries to scrub and brush and dress. The cold water makes her feel tingly, and hungry, but she rolls her tarp and closes her pack without eating, stuffing the sandwich in her pocket. Soon there is another clatter of dishes, and the man has set his plate on a table beside the window, and is sitting down where he can look out at the willow tree.

"Guess we'll have to wait," Karen whispers.

"Yes," Tom says, settling down.

Karen unwraps the sandwich and offers Tom half. He shakes his head.

The man takes a long time to eat. At first he begins to read a newspaper and the children think they might slip away without being seen, but then he glances up sharply. There is a rustle in the tree overhead, and a mockingbird begins to scold.

"It's scolding us," Karen whispers, ready to run.

"Maybe not," Tom says. "And the man won't know that, anyway. He'll think it's just making a racket. But he's watching, all right. Be very still."

Karen doesn't need to be told.

The bird makes an awful clatter, and Karen wonders if it is going to fly down and attack them. Maybe it has a nest nearby. The man continues to stare, until finally he pushes back his chair and gets up. The children wait, silent. The mockingbird screams furiously.

31

Then the back door opens, and the man comes out, still wiping his mouth. He is bearded and badly needs a haircut. He has narrow eyes. "He was in the inn last night," Tom whispers. Karen nods briefly. He is

coming toward the tree. Halfway there he stops and leans down. Karen holds her breath.

The man picks up a rock. Tom's face turns pale. Before the children can move the man has put back his arm and heaved the rock. There is a clatter above them, and squawking. Through the branches of the tree the mockingbird falls to Karen's feet and lies still. The man waits a minute, staring into the tree as if he intends to come after the bird, but then there is the rumble of a car on the road, a horn honks, and he goes into the house.

The bird lies quite still. Its eyes are closed, but as Tom picks it up its wings flutter. Tom holds it so it will not struggle, and tries to find a wound.

While they are examining the bird the horn honks again, the front door of the house opens, and the man goes down the steps and gets into the car and drives away. There is no other sound from the house. The children breathe a sigh.

"I can't find a thing wrong," Tom says, stroking the bird's head gently. The bird is now alert and watching them, not trying to move. "I think it was only stunned. Let's put it down." He slips quietly out from under the tree, and kneeling, sets the bird on the ground. The bird looks at him, cocks its head, and hops a few steps, watching Tom with one eye. It shakes its tail, flutters a little, then leaps into the sky and is gone. A minute later it is back, sitting on the roof of the house, scolding as before. Tom laughs. "Let's go," he says, "while we have the chance." They both look at the windows for further signs of life, but they see none.

"Before we do," Karen says, "there's a peach tree in the back yard, see?"

"It's risky enough, without going back there. There might be someone else home," Tom says. "Besides, that's stealing."

"They're ripe," Karen says. "Must be an early one."

Tom shakes his head.

"If I go close to the house I can't be seen from the windows. There are some on the ground, near the porch."

"They'll be bruised."

"Maybe not badly."

"All right, Karen, I'll go."

"No. Let me. You watch, and whistle if someone comes."

Tom frowns, but agrees.

As Tom watches the house and the road, Karen slips out and dashes for the house, crouching. She goes along it quickly, silently, until she reaches the rear corner. On the roof the mockingbird still scolds. Karen looks around the corner, then slips out to where the peaches lie, filling her pockets and blouse with the best ones, then scurrying back to the corner of the house.

Just then there is the noise of a car on the road. Karen huddles next to the house, not moving. But the car goes by, and when its sound is fainter she rounds the house and runs, doubled over, to the tree, bursting through the branches just as another car is heard. Tom frowns at her. "We could have been caught," he says.

While the car is approaching, the children put the peaches in their packs, slip the packs on, and get ready to run. Tom is still frowning, Karen pale. The excitement of stealing peaches has not lasted, and she is growing frightened.

This car, too, passes and goes on, and the children, listening for only a second, make a dash for the road and cross over into a thick clump of trees, walking briskly. They travel for a long way before they come back to the edge of the road once more. When they do, the last houses are behind them and the land ahead is rolling and green, here and there dotted with patches of yellow broom and clumps of dark-green trees. Away to the left the sea sparkles in the sun.

The children sit on an old stump behind a patch of tall wild barley, and share their stolen peaches, peeling them with Tom's knife.

"It is stealing," Tom says, enjoying the peach.

"I know," Karen says. "But at least not from a nice person. I wonder if the bird will be all right?"

"I'm sure it will," Tom says. "What a stupid thing to do. I wonder what it is about those people, and that inn. I'm glad we didn't stay."

"Yes," Karen says, peeling another peach.

As they come out onto the road again the sun is

warming the earth and swarms of tiny gnats have begun to hover close to the ground. From the trees flocks of brown wrens are swooping and darting after them, making a shrill chatter.

"If I were a bird," Karen says, "no one would know that I had run away from home. And I wouldn't need money, either."

"Nor a job," Tom says. "And what about me?"

"You'd be a bird, too." Karen giggles, suddenly turning giddy and flapping her arms wildly, hopping down the road and frightening everything around her. The birds stop their feasting and fly off a good distance to watch, screaming a warning to others.

Tom follows her, grinning. "No one will hire you if they see you doing that," he chides.

"No one did see," Karen says with a giggle.

"The birds did. Look at them."

"And they have gone," Karen says, ashamed of herself.

But the birds come back as the children follow the road more sedately. Ahead of them a tangle of yellow blooms stands beside the road. Tom picks a small bouquet for Karen, making a mocking bow. They do not fight much, this brother and sister. Not the way they used to. They remember, too often, that there is no one to scold them for it.

CHAPTER

4

Karen sighs and walks backward up the hill, looking off at the sea and nearly falling, then skips down the other side. Two plow horses in a pasture snort and watch her with ears thrust forward.

Someone else, quite close, is watching too.

Along the wide beach there are piles of driftwood, and beside one of these are the remains of a fire. Near this lies a blackened coffee can, and a long smooth trough dug in the sand, where someone has recently slept.

Now, fed and washed in the sea, the tramp has come out onto the road behind the children. He is much more heavily bearded than the men from the Black Turtle, white-bearded, and he carries a khaki pack like those of the children.

THE SAND PONIES

He sees Karen and Tom on the road ahead of him and he steps back into the trees and continues on his way at their speed, seeing, but unseen.

As the children top another hill they are close to the sea once more, and away in the rolling valley ahead of them a wisp of smoke rises from a farmhouse. "We will try there," Tom says. They start down, but before they are halfway to the valley the brightness of the morning has gone and a wind is knifing across the hills, bringing rain clouds with it.

The brilliant green of the fields has turned to dark jade, and the sea is steel-colored. "We'd better find shelter," Tom says, leading Karen away from the road and down a steep little valley where a stream sparkles. "There is a shed of some kind back in there; maybe it is deserted. It's going to rain hard when it starts."

The tramp, too, had thought of the shelter, earlier, when the clouds first started to form. It is deserted, sure, he knows that, but as the children head that way he draws back and starts for a cave higher up the hill that flanks the valley. He can keep dry there and watch the shelter below. He has not been to the cave before, nor to the shed either, but he knows of them, as do all hobos who come this way, from those who have passed before.

As the children follow an overgrown path along

the edge of the stream a roar of thunder makes them hurry, and soon they are pulling open the sagging door of the shack. There is a scurry inside and a mouse runs out, leaving its nest behind.

The roof looks as if it might keep off rain, and the three walls seem good. The rear wall is missing altogether, and in its place a thick cluster of straight young trees stands guard. Beyond these the hill rises up.

There is a broken chair in the shack, a pile of rubbish, and an old broom from which the mouse has taken straws, as have generations of mice before him.

The children put down their packs and, as it is not raining yet, go outside to explore.

The stream bubbles invitingly, and they drink and wash. Below them is a boggy place, and in it, thick as grass, is a great stand of cattails. Karen grins broadly, as does Tom, and the children scramble down and begin to cut off the few green heads which shine among the brown ones, and to fill their shirts with them.

When they have all they can reach they start toward the shack once more, but suddenly they turn and are off up the stream in the other direction, for they have seen a patch of bright orange shining there.

The tramp, from his cave, watches the children with interest.

When they have gathered a quantity of day-lily buds they begin to dig for the roots, and when their shirts are full and the first drops of rain are beginning to fall they hurry back to the shed.

Tom stretches a tarp between some trees, clears the ground, and begins to build a fire. Karen takes a quart can from her pack, removes her extra clothes from it, and fills it in the stream. The rain is coming harder now, but the fire is going and sheltered by the tarp, and soon the water is boiling. First the washed lily bulbs are put in, then the cattails, and last of all, the lily buds.

When their meal is cooked the children put out the fire and take their dinner to the shed, closing the door behind them. Reaching in with sticks to spear the food, they are soon fed and warmed as the rain pelts hard outside.

I wonder how they knew to do all that, thinks the tramp.

"It was not as good without butter and salt, the way Mamma used to fix it," Karen says.

"It was plenty good," Tom answers. "Could've used some wild onion, though."

"And meat," Karen says.

"Wonder if there are fish in the stream."

"Hmm, I wonder."

They have finished their meal with peaches, put up Tom's wet tarp at the back of the shack to fend off rain, and are stretched out on Karen's tarp, heads on their packs, listening to the rain drum on the wooden roof.

"I wonder where that poor mouse went," Karen says.

"Under the floor, probably. He'll not get wet."

"I hope not."

"When the rain is over I'm going down to see if that ranch will hire me."

"I'm to stay here?" Karen raises her head and stares at him.

"Would you mind? I think I'd have a better chance alone. They wouldn't be so suspicious. I could tell them about you after I got the job. If I get one. That way, I could see what they are like first. Would you mind staying alone?"

"I guess not. Let's see when it stops raining."

But it does not stop. It rains the rest of the afternoon, and all night, and though they have had a good meal, the children are quite hungry by morning. When Karen wakes, the sky has cleared but the trees drip steadily. Tom is down the stream, fishing with the line and hook from his pack. Karen sees where he has dug worms, and sees that he has caught nothing yet.

She goes upstream to wash, but soon comes running back, making signs to Tom with her hands, and darts into the shack to get a tarp.

The tramp watches them. He has breakfasted on beans and bread.

As Tom goes upstream with the tarp Karen fills the water can and begins to clear the fire spot of its

wet refuse. She covers the ground with stones, brings the dry trash from the shed, and soon has a fire going.

When Tom comes back the tarp is looped around something heavy. Karen goes off downstream. This is Tom's job; though he hates to do it, she hates it worse, and he is left to cook the four crayfish, plunging them alive into the boiling water. Karen returns when the cooking is done and the children have their breakfast. "You can sure eat 'em, for not cooking them," Tom kids her.

"I found them," retorts Karen.

The tramp still watches.

The sun is well up when they finish. Tom puts on his clean shirt and looks across the valley to the ranch, then looks at Karen.

"I'll wash your shirt," she says, "and mine. If you don't come back by noon, though, I'm coming after you."

"All right," he says, turning to leave. It is then that he sees the tramp sitting behind a rock at the mouth of the cave. He is almost hidden, but the sunlight catches his hand. Tom looks away, then goes back into the shed and tells Karen to put on her pack.

Soon both children are following the stream to the valley, the shadows of clouds dappling the fields below them.

"It gives me chills to think of that man," Karen says as they stand on the last hill, looking down at the ranch. "What do you suppose he was doing there? Why was he watching us?"

"I don't know," Tom answers. "I didn't have time to take a good look. I didn't want him to know I saw him. All I really got a look at was his hand."

"You couldn't have been mistaken?"

"No. I saw enough to know there was a man there."

"Well, shall we try the ranch?"

"Yes."

"Or shall I stay here?"

"No. We'll stay together."

The tramp sees them now only as tiny specks down the valley.

Overhead, someone else watches the children. In the sky a great black crow glides silently, spiraling on a draft of air, watching them go down the road to the lane, and down the lane to the big front door. The crow caws loudly.

The ranch house is tall and square and white, with a deep porch that has two faded rockers on it. The door is solid and dark and the front windows heavily curtained. The whole place is strangely quiet. No dog barks, no chickens squawk. There is not a living thing in sight, not even a cat.

Tom knocks and waits. There is no answer. He knocks again.

"They're all away somewhere," Karen says finally. "Let's go, Tom."

"Go where?"

"On up the road, away from here. A ranch shouldn't be so quiet. I don't like it."

"I don't like it with that man around," Tom says, glancing back at the hills. "I thought . . . well, I'd feel safer if we could sleep here, tonight, anyway. Listen, Karen, we can tell them we're on a walking trip. People do do that. We can say we'd like to rest and earn our board for a few days, if they need help."

"Tell who?"

"Well, they're bound to be back. You can't leave a ranch very long. There must be cows to milk, stock to feed."

"It's awfully quiet, Tom."

"Let's go see."

They round the side of the house and head toward the barn. In the fields alfalfa and grain are growing, but the crops look weedy and are not well cared for. There is no stock in the corrals. The barn is dim and does not smell right. There are no cows in the stanchions, and the boxes farther on are empty.

The children gaze about them. "Let's get out of here," Karen says. "I don't like it. It's not natural."

Tom is looking at the farm tractor, the harrow, and the plow. "These are used, Karen."

"Well, of course! We saw crops. But no animals, Tom? On a ranch?"

Suddenly there is a loud banging at the back of the barn. Both children start. Karen takes Tom's hand. "Let's go, Tom."

"Wait." The banging comes again. Then a series of bangs, and a snort. "That's a horse pawing his stall, Karen!"

CHAPTER

5

In the dimmest part of the barn the pawing starts again and the children hurry toward it. In a dark stall a small roan mare snorts and leaps away as the children look over the door. The mare wheels and lets her heels fly, her ears tight to her head. Then, as the children do not enter, she peers around at them, teeth bared, and turns to press herself against the wall, ears still flat, eyes wild.

"Phew," Karen says. Both children's nostrils wrinkle. The stall is wet and mucky. There is no straw and no feed, and the mare is very thin and bedraggled. The children can see where some hay has been dumped on the wet ground and she has eaten it, leaving only a few specks of grain in the mud. There is no water bucket in the stall, and the mare is gaunt from thirst as well as thin.

Tom has walked away and is looking in the next stall. There is another pony there, head down, thinner than the mare, every rib showing. He, too, is roan, and in the third stall a small gray mare stands and looks at the children hopefully, but when Tom opens the door she lays back her ears and leaps wildly at him. He slams the door in her face.

The children look at each other. Karen goes to find a grain room or some feed, Tom to find water and a bucket.

"The water first," Tom says, bringing the bucket finally. "I'm afraid we'll bloat them, otherwise."

He hangs the bucket gingerly over the first mare's stall, but she will not approach until he has leaned down and set it on the ground inside and backed away. Then she drinks all that he has given her.

"Let's get them out of these wet stalls," Tom says. "Probably have thrush. Did you find any feed?"

"No. But there's plenty in the fields."

"What kind of a place is this?" Tom says as he digs in an open trunk for a decent halter.

Karen looks at him. "She's awful mean, Tom."

"I know. Open those stalls over there. They're dry."

Karen does as he says, then stands back to head the mare off if she should get loose. He opens the door and the mare lunges at him, teeth bared. He steps back, slapping her with the halter, then steps in and toward her again.

At this minute there is a loud roar as a truck drives up to the barn, the driver gunning the motor. Karen moves to the side of the barn and Tom closes the mare's door. The children try to get out the back door, but it is bolted from outside. "There is a side door," Tom whispers. They hurry around to it as the truck door slams, and open it and go through just as they hear voices.

Instead of the bright outdoors they are met with

total darkness as they shut the door softly behind them.

They listen at the door, but can hear nothing. "I smell mice," Karen whispers.

"And grain," Tom says. "This is the grain room, Karen."

"My gosh, I'll bet there're a million mice in here."

"You didn't mind that one in the shed."

"Well, he could get out! I don't like being shut in with them."

"Stand still, they won't hurt you."

"All right. But you do the same. Don't stir them up."

Tom has his ear to the door. "Shhh," he whispers. The voices are nearer.

"Here, put these packages in the catch, Ed." It is a gruff man's voice. Then, shouting, "Get that truck in here, Tip."

There is a mutter the children can't make out, then the first voice again: "No, not till we've got those critters out of the truck. Then you'll get the stuff."

The second voice is louder this time. ". . . get us all in a mess with this, Charley! What're you trying to prove?"

The truck starts up and the children hear it backing into the barn, stopping, finally, very close to them. "Open them stalls, Ed."

"They are open."

"Well, what the . . ."

"Come on, come on, ain't got all night." This is a new voice. It must be the one called Tip.

"Shut up and come on." Charley's voice again.

There is the sound of metal, then a thud. "Okay, tail gate's down. Get a move on," Tip says.

There is a good deal of stomping and banging, some cursing, and after a long time the children hear a stall door close, then the same sounds over again, and another door shut. "Okay, here's your package. Now clear out of here," Charley growls.

"But what're you doing this for, Charley?" Tip sounds as if he is standing right by the door to the feed room. Karen finds Tom's hand in the darkness and holds it tight.

"Listen, you guys got what you came for. This is my business. I'm gonna master those critters. Say they've never been broke, do they? Well, I'll break 'em, all right." Charley hacks and spits loudly.

"Ain'tcha gonna feed 'em, Charley?" Ed says.

"Naw, feed 'em later. Make 'em gentle, go without long enough. Give me a hand, get those ropes off 'fore you go, Ed."

"Not me, man. You're crazy. Them ponies'll kill ya."

"I said, help me get those ropes off. You, too, Tip."

There is some muttering, growing softer as the

men move away, then a good deal of banging, some dull thuds, swearing, and finally, "Did 'e hurt ya, Charley?"

"Didn't hurt me, the little ———! Better clear out of here, now. Got your directions?"

"Yeah."

"Okay. Get going."

The voices cease, the truck starts and drives away, and soon the barn is quiet once more.

"My gosh," Karen whispers. The children listen for a long time, but they cannot tell whether Charley has left or stayed in the barn. "We'd better not go out," Karen says softly. "I think he's still there."

"Maybe I can see if I open the door a little. We've got to get out of here before he decides to feed them."

"He won't. Didn't you hear him?"

"Yes," Tom says with disgust. "I'm going to look, Karen."

"Be careful."

Tom inches the door open until a crack of light shows through. "I don't see him. I'm going to look around the corner. You stay here." Karen doesn't say anything.

In a minute Tom is back. "He must have gone in the house. I can hear water running."

"Clear from here?"

"Yes. I think the kitchen must be on this side. It sounds like it's running into a sink or a tub."

"But he won't give the horses a drink."

THE SAND PONIES

Tom shakes his head. "Listen, Karen, something's . . ." Just at that minute they hear a car drive up and Tom jumps back into the feed room.

There is the slam of a car door, faint, as if it comes from near the house, then silence. For a long time the children listen, but hear nothing. "We could leave now, maybe," Karen says finally.

"What about the horses?"

"Are you thinking we should turn them loose?"

"Aren't you?"

"Yes, but I thought you'd say that was stealing!"

"You know better than that!" Tom growls.

"I'm sorry. I'm just edgy, I guess."

"I know. So am I. But we aren't leaving without turning those ponies loose. We may have to wait until tonight, when we won't be seen."

"But what will happen if we turn them loose, sick like that?"

"They'll eat. They'll have a better chance than here. Didn't you get the idea they were wild?"

"Yes. I wonder how he caught them. And wild ponies, Tom? Here? I never heard of such a thing."

"It does seem funny. But everything about this place is funny. No stock. Only crops. Maybe the horses were let run loose on the grazing land until they got too wild to handle."

"Well, whatever it is, you're right. We can't leave without turning them loose," Karen says.

"Shh, I hear something."

Outside there is a low murmur of voices, a sound
as if a bolt is being slid, then more talking, louder.
This time there is a woman's voice. "Listen, Charley,
I want that last bundle moved right away. And Tip's
got to work tonight. So do you. Put this stuff in the
feed room till you're ready for it."

Karen and Tom slip quickly away from the door,
and feeling their way, crouch behind the grain sacks.
There is a soft scuttling, and Karen stiffens. There
are mice there, all right. She bites her lip.

Just in time the children are hidden. The door
opens, and a dark figure heaves a heavy package into
the room. Behind him, in the patch of light, stands a
thin, dark woman. Then the door slams shut.

"Tom, that was the woman from the Black Turtle!"
Karen whispers.

"Yes, and I thought I recognized the man, too,
from the bar."

"My gosh."

They can hear little else from this spot behind the
grain sacks, and finally they creep to the door again,
but all is quiet outside.

"They said tonight," Karen whispers. "We've got
to get out of here."

"Listen, Karen, if I can get that back door open we
can take the horses out that way. There must be a
side door. I'm going to try to get outside."

"Tom?"

"What?"

"There wasn't any other door. Maybe *this* was the side door, once."

"You mean they closed it in? I'll have a look." He begins to feel along the wall. Mice scurry toward Karen, confused. Karen holds her breath. One runs over her foot. They're only little, she says to herself. They are more frightened than I. That doesn't help much, but soon Tom is back.

"There's a door back there in the corner," he says. "I slid the bolt."

"But the ponies'll never drive through the feed room."

"No. I'll go around and unbolt the back barn door from the outside."

"Now, while it's light?"

"The sun will start to set soon. When it's dusk I'll go. Meantime, I'm going to feed those ponies."

"Now?"

"Yes, now."

Karen knows better than to argue with this.

"Help me rip this bag open, Karen. They'll have to eat on the ground."

"My gosh, Tom, there might be mouse nests in there."

"All right." Tom takes out his knife and starts to cut the sack. Soon Karen is helping him.

Finally, carrying a good amount of grain wrapped in a piece of sacking, Tom opens the door and peers into the dim barn. The way is clear.

He goes to the corner and looks around. The barn is quite empty. Karen holds her breath until she has heard him dump grain into five stalls, making a small shooshing noise each time and riling the ponies until she is afraid they will be heard from the house. Finally he is back with her, the door tightly shut behind him. "It's cooling off a little; the sun is low. It won't be long."

"Did you see anything?"

"No one. No noise from the house. The new ponies are something! Both roan, both small. Funny. Like mountain horses. These are fat and nice, but devils! Ran at me when I put the grain in. Cute as they can be."

"Suppose they'll run at us when we let them out?"

"Maybe. Until they see they're free."

"Yes."

"I'm hungry. Any peaches left?"

"Two."

"Let's have them."

"What do you suppose is in that package?"

"Maybe I can tell by the shape." Tom feels around until he finds it, then announces, "Cans of something, small, but heavy. They have labels, if only we could see."

"Here," Karen says. She has peeled a peach for him. "How'll we know when it's dark?"

"The mice'll dance."

"Oh, hush," she says, and giggles.

"I hear something," Tom says.

Karen listens. "They're coming back. Oh, Tom, what if they see the grain?"

"Shhh."

"I hear walking."

"A bolt slid," Tom whispers, then stiffens. There is a squeal from one of the horses, then crashing and a slam, then swearing; a good deal of swearing.

There is nothing more for a minute; then they hear a soft groan, and minutes later, a slow scuffling walk toward the house.

"That pony hurt him," Karen says, delighted.

"I hope he hurt him good!"

"Listen, Tom, if we let them out back, won't there be fences?"

"My gosh, there might be. It'll have to be the front."

"Oh, boy."

"Well, we'll have to try. We'll let the sick ones out first, then the new ones—they may drive the others."

"I don't think they'll *need* much driving."

"I'm going to see how dark it is." Tom leaves her and makes his way to the outside door. He opens it and peers out. The thin slit of light is paler. "The sun's going down. It won't be long," he whispers as he returns.

"I'm sure hungry."

"Eat some grain."

"With mice in it?"

"We could cook some later."

"That's not a bad idea. I guess if we cooked it long enough it would be all right." Karen begins to scoop grain into a piece of sacking, and soon they have a small package of oats tied up and put in Tom's pack. "Tom, see how dark it is now."

"Okay." He looks again. The light is somewhat dimmer. "It's clouding up. It's going to rain."

"Maybe they'll stay in the house, then."

"I wouldn't count on it. I'm going to try now. If I can get the ponies moving, we can go out this way. Listen! The rain's started! Maybe it will hide us; and the horses."

"Won't they get confused when they get outside the barn?"

"There are fences on both sides of the drive. They'll have to go right by the house, but it's a straight shot to the road, and with the rain, maybe they won't be heard. It's coming down harder, hear it?"

"Let's go," Karen says, lifting her pack. "Going to be wet out there!"

"You stay here until I get the ponies started."

"Oh, no."

"All right." Tom puts on his own pack and unbolts the door.

CHAPTER

6

It is much darker in the barn and the children can work without being seen from the house. The rain pelts noisily on the roof, hiding the sound of the door bolts. Quickly the doors are opened—first the sick pony, who won't leave and must be driven out by Tom, and then stands, uncertain, in the alleyway of the barn. "I hate to send him out into the rain," Tom whispers, "but it would be worse to leave him." Next the two mares are let out, one leaping at Tom, teeth bared, before she is driven off, then the two new ones. All four, seeing the open door, break into a wild run toward it, sweeping the dazed one with them. "He's not too sick to run," Tom says.

Even through the sound of the rain the children can hear the clatter of hoofs on the drive, and suddenly the back door of the house is thrown open and

a figure rushes out—but too late. The horses are already by and heading for the road.

"Hurry, my gosh, hurry, Karen. Here they come!" The children rush back into the grain room, shove the opened sack against the door, and race for the door in the corner, mice scattering. There is no way to bolt this door from outside. They crouch beside it for a minute to get their bearings. "Come on," Tom says. There is a fence running beside the barn and tall grain growing on the other side. The children slide under the fence and crawl into the grain until they are hidden. "If we creep," Tom whispers, "they'll see the grain moving."

They lie still, listening. There is silence for a minute, then faint shouting from the barn as the man and woman argue, voices getting louder and louder through the drumming of rain.

"I told you not to keep those stupid ponies."

"Aw, shut up, Kay! You ain't got . . ."

"Come on, Karen," Tom cuts in. The children crawl out from the field and race for the road.

Past the house they go—the ponies have fled—down the lane, completely exposed. The rain is getting harder, but through it they hear footsteps running behind them, then shouting. The children run faster still, panting; their packs seem heavier, pulling at their shoulders as they try to keep their footing on the muddy lane.

When they reach the road there is a great clap of thunder, and the rain increases to a torrent, a solid curtain of water, drenching them, but hiding them, too. The lane, the house are hidden. The children run on through the cloudburst and down the road as fast as they can go.

The rain pelts into their faces until they can hardly see, and their clothes are soaked and heavy. Then the wind comes, driving needles of water against them like knives, but they keep running, fighting through it, stumbling over rocks, exhausted, winded, for what seems like an eternity. Finally, hearts pounding, they drop into a ditch at the side of the road. The rain beats at them, sloshing into the ditch around them; but the rain has saved them.

They listen. There is no other sound but the rain. It has grown quite dark. They wait in the ditch a long time, breathing hard, until Karen begins to shiver with the cold. Tom feels her hand. "We've got to get shelter somewhere." He gets up.

"We've the tarps."

"Not enough. Come on. At least we can keep warmer if we're moving."

"I can't see."

"The road's here." He pulls her up. "Come on."

They walk and walk, still pelted with rain. "I wonder if the ponies got away all right," Karen says.

"Of course they did. All but the sick one, maybe."

"Poor, poor thing."

"We did what we could. He would have died there."

It seems as if they have been walking in the pounding rain forever. They are numb with cold. Karen stumbles. "I can't go any farther, Tom. Let's just lie down in the ditch and put the tarps over us."

"We'll freeze there. It's better to keep walking."

"I can't."

"Yes, you can." They go on.

"Where is the road going? Did you notice when we came to the ranch?" she asks finally.

"Past the ranch toward the ocean, I remember that. We're going down, I'm sure. I don't remember any houses or anything."

"Toward the ocean? Would there be caves there?"

"Maybe, but how safe from the tide?"

"Yes. Well, morning will come sometime, I guess." A tear is sliding down her nose, mixed with the rain. She can't help it. She is so cold she aches, and hungry; lost. Even Uncle George's would be better than this.

Or would it, Karen?

Suddenly there are lights on the road ahead of them. A car is coming. They crouch in the ditch. The car takes a long time to get to them, but finally it passes in a whirling of mud and water, and is gone.

"I saw something," Tom says. Karen is really crying now. She huddles against herself and can't seem to stop. "Karen!" He shakes her. "Karen, I saw a house!"

"What difference does it make? We can't go to a house. We can't go anywhere!" She dissolves into helpless sobbing.

Tom feels like crying, too. But he does not. Someone has to get them out of his. He lifts her gently until she is on her feet. "Come on, Karen!" he commands. She follows him.

Walking seems almost impossible—a mechanical action—one foot, then the other, right foot, left foot, right, left, which is which? On and on; wet, always been wet, cold. Left foot, right foot, something pulling her along; Tom? Rain in her face, darkness. Blind. I am blind, Karen thinks. The earth is ended. Left foot, right, then, "Come on, Karen, down here." Tom's voice? Who knows? She is too tired and numb to care.

CHAPTER

7

It is a long time later. Karen wakes. Her clothes are off and she is wrapped in something smelly. Paint? Yes, paint smell. It is a dim place, and she thinks she is back at Uncle George's. She looks around. Everything is strange; she can't make it out at all. On the other side of the dark little room, Tom sleeps. Their clothes are hung against a grayish wall; concrete? There is a wooden rooflike thing overhead, slanting down on one side. She stares at it. Light seeps through around the edges. She raises herself on one elbow and looks. They are in a cellar. The wooden roof is an overhead door. It is latched from inside. The cellar is small and warm. She listens. Outside a rooster crows. She closes her eyes. Warm. She is lying on something soft. She sleeps again.

This time she dreams.

THE SAND PONIES

She is walking along a cliff above the sea. The path is grassy, and yellow mustard fields stretch away to hills which lie in shadow beneath dark clouds. Below the cliff the sea sucks and beats at a ribbon of sand.

The path wanders a little and hugs the cliff's edge. Gulls cry. The air is heady with salt. A small brown lizard suns on a rock, and does not run when she strokes him. Buttercups grow by the lizard's rock, and a snail sleeps.

The path drops steeply down the side of the cliff. She follows it. Grains of sand glint like diamonds at her feet.

Black sea caves in an outcropping of rock receive onslaughts of water, are filled by them, then stand empty, dripping, until the next crashing wave.

She stands with her back to the cliff, enchanted by the writhing of the sea; she is part of the sea. A gull sweeps overhead, silvered in the sunlight. Silent.

She climbs the wet rocks and watches the tide pools fill and empty. Transparent green swells explode and fall away, leaving jewels of wetness behind them, leaving clusters of bright shells bedded in green seaweed; leaving small red crabs scuttling.

The sea grows wilder, hurling spray in her face. A seagull screams. The tide has risen and the sand is covered. A knife-edged wind tugs at her hair. Water foams wildly among the rocks.

Fog begins to roll over the sea, crushing the sun. Karen turns back to the cliff, but it is a long way away.

Wind whips at her, waves break nearer. Clinging, clinging to the wet rock, slipping, she cannot get close to the cliff. Fog grows thick around her. She is slipping, climbing frantically.

Then the fog closes in around her, below her, hiding the sea. The crash of waves is muffled. The fog swirls up around the cliff's edge. It writhes and dances, white and cold and eerie, like clammy hands, pushing closer, closer to her. She starts to run; but she is running on the great carpet of fog; running, running across it. She runs until she is surrounded by it and cannot see the land. She is lost and alone. She stops and turns, but as she does she begins to sink into the fog—deeper, deeper. She struggles.

Then the fog is gone. She is standing once more in the field of mustard. The day is warm and still. The sea below is blue and very calm. A cricket sings. A bird calls. A small green beetle watches her. She tastes a yellow mustard flower. She looks along the path, down at the empty beach.

But the beach is not empty. Something, someone, is there.

When she wakes she cannot remember. She cannot remember who was there on the beach, looking up at her.

The cellar is lighter now, as if the sun is well up, but Tom still sleeps. Karen gets up and feels her clothes, knowing they will still be wet. She gets her others from her pack and puts them on. There is no water for washing, or for drinking. She is very thirsty. She begins to look around. The cellar is not as small as she first thought. Steps lead down to a darker, larger part below. It is dim, but going carefully, Karen climbs down.

Bags of potatoes and carrots sit in one corner, and shelves of canned food line the walls. Karen reads the labels, written in a small, neat hand, and picks out a jar of peaches. By the time Tom wakes she has the lid off, and has eaten half of them. "We can leave money for it," she says as he looks at her. She hands him the jar.

As Tom eats they begin to hear little scratching sounds overhead, then clucking; there is a woman's voice, calling chickens, and a dog barks nearby.

Karen grins. "This one has livestock, all right. We'd better get down where it's dark." They move to the farthest corner of the cellar, behind some large barrels.

"We may have to stay here until nighttime," Tom says. "Unless we decide to ask for a job!"

"Wouldn't they think it strange if we came out of their cellar?"

"Yes, I guess they would." He grins.

"Maybe we'll hear them talking and find out what kind of people they are."

"Yes, maybe."

"Tom?"

"Hmmm?"

"What do you think happened to Kippy and Tolly and Ginger and Rex?"

"What made you think of that now?"

"I don't know; a dream I had, I guess; or maybe it was the ponies last night. I hope they got away safely."

"So do I."

"But what do you think, Tom? Do you think our horses are safe, too?"

"No one would pay good money for them, then neglect them. Kippy probably has some little girl to put up with, and maybe Tolly has a boy. They're all right, Karen. They're not ownerless and homeless like those ponies."

"I guess you're right. But I wish I knew; I do wish I knew. I don't know what it was about that dream, but it made me so restless; as if something, or someone, were waiting for me—as if something were going to happen. I do wish I knew where Kippy was, and if he's taken care of."

Tom squirms around to make himself more comfortable, then both children hush. Overhead, a young boy is shouting, there is the sound of trotting; then the cellar door creaks, and the boy, very close, cries, "Papa, Papa, I saw them!"

"Don't shout. I'm right here, Jerry." The voice is so close that the children stare at each other. Has the man been there all the time, perhaps sitting on the cellar door? Has he heard them talking? Tom shakes his head. He couldn't have heard their whispers. The man continues, "Here, loosen the cinch if you're going to let him stand. Is he hot?"

"No, Papa." There is a pause. "Well, a little."

"Then walk him around while you tell me. What did you see?"

The boy's voice starts out loudly, but fades as he walks his horse, then comes clearer again, as if he is walking in a circle. "I saw the Sand Ponies, Papa! Down near the west pasture, down by the bog." Karen and Tom look at each other. "Big as life," the boy continues. "Big as life I saw them! We'll have luck for sure, won't we, Papa? But, Papa, they sure were skinny. They've always been so fat—it's been a good year for feed, too. Why were they so thin?"

"Were they?" There is a pause. "How many, Jerry? Could you count them?"

"Oh, sure. Just five of them. That does seem funny, now you think of it—never seen but the whole band together before, like that time in the ravine—but they sure were Sand Ponies, Papa."

"Sure?"

"Oh, sure! Four roans, one gray. Sand Ponies, sure. Little and short-coupled, ears back, all of 'em, when they saw me."

The man chuckles. "I'll saddle up old Doc and we'll go see. Seems mighty funny, just a few like that. And skinny. Could be they're sick, Jerry. Come on." The door creaks, and the children hear footsteps going away.

The next voice is a woman's—the same one that called the chickens. "Breakfast's ready, Joe, Jerry."

"Put it on the back of the stove, Nell. We're off after Sand Ponies," the man shouts.

"Sand Ponies? My goodness, where?"

"West pasture. Jerry says they look queer. Might be sick."

"Oh, dear. Best go right away. My! Poor, dear things. I'll set the breakfast back."

The children hear horses trotting off. "They *must* be the same ponies, Tom," Karen whispers.

"Yes. What did the boy say about bringing luck?"

" 'We'll have luck, sure,' or something like that."

"I wonder what he meant. Do you suppose they think those ponies are bewitched or something?" Tom says.

"Could be. But those men last night didn't think so."

"They were too mean to believe in anything." Tom is frowning.

"I wonder why they're called Sand Ponies. Sounds almost like a fairy name." Karen wriggles farther down behind the barrels. "I wonder where they came from."

Tom is folding his nearly dry clothes. "Pretty strange, all right. This sure isn't the kind of country where you'd expect to find wild horses."

"Yes, it is queer."

"Maybe they *are* fairy ponies, Karen!" he says, grinning.

"Maybe!"

A long time later the man and boy return, walking by the cellar and talking softly. The children hear a door close, then the woman's voice: "Oh, Joe. Oh, poor, poor thing. Whatever is wrong, do you think?"

"It's the sick one," Tom whispers.

"Come on, boy," the man says softly. "Come on there, so, boy, easy now, easy, boy, easy, slowly with the gate, Jerry, there, boy, there, now, close it gently,

Jerry. Ah, there now. Go and put some water on for mash, Nell."

"Shouldn't he be in a stall, Joe?"

"Don't think he'd do as well there; wild ones usually don't. Hurry, now." They hear the woman shut the door again. Later, when she returns, the children hear the three people talking softly, but cannot make out the words. Finally, after a long time, the man and boy come to sit on the cellar door once more.

"You think that's all, Papa? Just hungry?"

"Hard to tell for sure, but I think so. Those ponies have been shut up someplace, nasty rope burns like that. Like to catch the dirty coward who did it."

"Rope burns on all of them, Papa. How could anyone? Fresh burns on those fat ones, like they were just caught."

"Yes. Sure would like to know why."

"To sell?"

"No money in those little things."

"Then why?"

"Meanness, maybe."

They are silent for a while; then Jerry says, "Look, Papa, he's starting to eat."

"Good boy, go to it, boy," the man says softly.

Karen and Tom look at each other and smile. "Like to work here?" Tom whispers.

"Oh, yes. They're nice, Tom."

"It's pretty close to that ranch, Karen."

"Would they recognize us?"

"From the Black Turtle, if not from the ranch."

"Yes. What do you suppose was going on there? Besides the ponies, I mean?"

"I don't know, but it sure did sound funny. Something crooked, I'll bet."

"But what?" Karen asks.

"Stealing? Smuggling? I don't know, but I think we should tell the police."

"But, Tom, how *can* we? Won't they wonder what we were doing there?"

"When we come to a town, why can't we just phone the police? They wouldn't have to know who we were."

"I guess we could. But what if it turned out to be nothing?"

"No harm done, then."

"Yes."

"Karen, let's fix ourselves a good meal down here—later, figure out how much it would cost and leave the money—then get some sleep and leave before it's light. We know this place is here, and we can come back to it if we want. We won't starve, and if we do come back to ask for a job, we'd look a lot better coming from the north."

"Getting the wanderlust?"

"Maybe. Made out okay so far, haven't we?"

"And we will long as the cattails hold out."

"And the fruit cellars."

"Help me pick out a meal," Karen says, getting up and going to the shelves.

They choose raspberries, raw carrots, and a jar of butter beans with ham. "Aren't you supposed to heat these things before you eat them?" Tom asks.

"The berries would be all right, with sugar, I think, but I don't know, maybe we shouldn't eat the beans." Karen puts them back on the shelf.

"Sure look good, though."

"I know. But let's see what else. How about . . . oh, look, here's a cheese, Tom!"

"Well, that should be all right. We can cut it and take the rest with us. Are there more?"

"Yes, more. We won't be taking the last."

"Well, add everything up. I'll put the money here." She does, then lies down, with her head on her pack. "I wish I had a book," she says. "This would be a lovely place to read."

"You can't see very well."

"But it's so quiet."

"Yes, not a bad place at all, if we had a lamp down here."

"Go ask for one!" she says.

"Smart!"

"Really, though, what's wrong with a cellar? Warm in winter, cool in summer, quiet. Could make a real nice house."

"Well, I like to look at the sky, too."

"Look, Tom, if you took that door out and put in

glass, you could have light and look right at the sky."

"Yes, you could. Part of the house could be on top. There could be steps here on the high part going up to a living room and kitchen. Down here could be bedrooms, and a quiet study."

Karen takes a small note pad from her pack. "Got a pencil?"

"Sure." He hands it to her.

Soon they are so engrossed in designing an underground house that the cellar has become quite dark and they are frowning, trying to see, before they finish.

They have heard little noise from above, but now the sounds of evening chores have begun, the clanging of a bucket, gates slamming, all the familiar noises. They sit quietly and listen.

Before the light is completely gone Karen cuts the cheese and opens the berries and Tom peels a few carrots. They dine royally, put their scraps in the jar, then spread out their tarps and coats behind the barrels.

"I hope I wake up," Tom says.

"I will," says Karen. "I want to wade in the ocean."

CHAPTER
8

Karen wakes very early. The cellar is dark; the dial
on Tom's watch, when she kneels to see, says three
o'clock. She dresses, opens a jar of peaches, then
wakes Tom.

As the children leave the cellar the farmyard lies
in moonlight all around them. "What about the dog?"
Karen whispers.

"He didn't bark when we came. I think he sleeps
in the house."

"Fine farm dog!"

"Be glad for it!"

"I am."

"I want to see the pony first," Tom says, heading
for the corral.

The little roan is standing, ears back, watching

them as they approach. "It's him, all right," Tom says. "He looks better."

"Yes. Look, his manger is clean, and his grain bucket."

"He'll be all right."

The children skirt the corral and head toward the road. Soon they are all alone with the night, a cold breeze from the sea blowing in their faces. As the dawn begins to come they can see early rabbits in the fields, and once they see a doe. "Maybe we'll see the Sand Ponies," Karen says.

"Maybe."

They watch the sun come up over the hills as they sit on a patch of high meadow above the sea. As the sky turns to pink a black shape glides and circles above them, cawing.

The crow has watched them come through a copse of trees and climb the hill to the meadow. He watches them eat their cheese, then soars into the sky to see what else moves so early in his fields.

Looking up at the crow and out at the sparkling sea, Karen thinks of home; of home and Kippy. Where are you, Kippy? she wonders. Where are you this morning?

It is some months earlier. Spring has come to the mountains, and a small buckskin horse lifts his head and gazes across a field where snow is melting. He is listening in vain for the pounding of the sea.

It has been a strange white winter. Kippy has never known heavy snow before; he doesn't like it. It is cold to the feet and legs, and there is nothing green for grazing, only hay. The man has been good enough to him, has fed him and left him alone. The other horses have fared less well this winter; they have been ridden, and worse, carried pack, while Kippy—too small, perhaps, or too disagreeable—has been left to himself.

But now it is spring. The snow is melting and the first green shoots are beginning to mingle their scent with the smell of wet earth.

In some creatures more than in others, the beginnings of spring, the first blades of new grass, start a longing beyond description for the fields of their early years.

So it is with Kippy. All the horses feel it, but for Kippy it is a driving need, a passion he cannot resist.

He grows restless, irritable. He angers easily and

drives the other horses away from his favorite spots in the field. His ears go back at the slightest provocation; and often he will stand gazing away to the northwest, chewing lazily, but with a strange wild look in his eye.

The other horses begin to avoid him; he frightens Tolly, who has been bred and is growing gentle and slow. She keeps away from him. Sometimes he runs at her and nips her flank. He does not know why, nor does she; she only knows it frightens her now, where it would not have before. She turns her back on him and lashes out in anger and fear. What does he want, Kippy, who has been her friend? These should be quiet days for her; she does not want to be disturbed. Ginger and Rex do not mind so much. Kippy is acting strangely, but they ignore him. After all, it is spring.

There are eight horses in the pasture. Besides Kippy, Tolly, Ginger, and Rex, there are two big race-track mares, crazy and mean, both in foal and their dispositions not improved by it. There is a pinto pony who is fat and lazy, and a small black mare who is old and turning gray. She keeps much to herself, away from the big mares, at peace with the world and avoiding trouble. But now that spring has come, even she has a gleam in her eye, a coltish look about her. Spring has come, and every creature feels the stir of it.

Kippy most of all. The urge is driving him; he cannot be still. Northwest, across the mountains, something is waiting for him. There the grass is greener, sweeter. There the ocean breezes blow.

He begins to work at one corner of the fence, out of sight of the house and barn. It is barbed wire, but he is wise to that. Slowly, every day, he leans between the strands, putting his weight on them. Slowly, every day, the wire stretches a little more, until finally, forced with a surge of impatience, it snaps. One wire gone, one wire to step over, one under. Pity the horse who gets caught in that broken wire.

Starting with Tolly and Ginger, Kippy begins to herd the horses together. He is not going alone across the mountains. He gets them moving with nips that leave marks on their rumps. Like a sheep dog he is, quick and willful. Next, Rex and the pony, then the old mare. He doesn't bother the two Thoroughbred mares. He will not attempt to drive them with the others.

Why are they so slow, these horses? It is spring, can't they smell it? Don't they know he is giving them freedom? They mill and resist him. Tolly fights back; she doesn't want freedom just now. Rex is more willing. Ginger doesn't understand.

The old mare doesn't want to go. *This* is her colthood pasture. She retires to her corner. Kippy drives the pony through with Ginger and Tolly and Rex, so that five of them go through the fence, go along the stream between the trees away from the ranch.

There is a long way to travel. It will take them many days, many weeks, but it is early spring, and the sea is calling Kippy home.

CHAPTER

9

The children sit in the meadow looking at the ocean
and watching the morning grow lighter. As the sun
breaks away from the hills and hangs like a red ball
in the sky they start down to the lower fields which
flank the sea.

There is one small grove to go through. A stream
enters it, coming out the other side to spill itself
into the ocean. "We'll have a drink," Tom says, and
they start down. Then they stop suddenly, for there
in the grove strange shapes are moving. It is too dark
in there to see what they are. The children watch for
a long time; then Karen whispers, "I think it's horses."

Tom nods and stands quietly, watching. As their
eyes grow more accustomed to the scene they are
sure of it. "There are no fences," Karen says. "It's not
a fenced pasture, Tom."

"Let's try to get closer," he says.

Down they go, looking as much like shadows as they can. But not enough like shadows. The horses begin to move around a little. The children stop still. The horses settle down. After a while the children move ahead again. They get a little farther this time; then suddenly the ponies come to life in a great swirl of movement, like birds taking wing, and are out and running across the meadow to the hills.

They are roans and grays, all of them.

They cross the meadow bunched close and melt into a patch of dunes where they can hardly be seen. Sand-colored ponies on the sand hills.

The children watch the ponies as they drift away over the dunes and into a valley, out of sight.

Karen sighs. "They were lovely."

Tom laughs. "Did you see the leader nip at them to make them run faster? Sand Devils, I'd call them."

"There must have been fifty, Tom."

"At least."

"I think they'll bring us luck!"

"Maybe."

The children go on down to the stream. Wherever the soft ground is bare of leaves, it is covered with small hoofprints. There is a nice horse smell about the place, mixed with eucalyptus. The ponies have muddied the water, and the children go farther up to drink, then return to explore. Karen finds three silver hairs on a bush and ties them into a knot around her finger. "A magic ring, to wish on," she says.

Tom smiles.

The crow returns and lands in a tree and caws at them.

The children leave the grove and start toward the sea. They follow a narrow path which goes to the edge of the cliff, then along it.

Suddenly Karen pauses. Farther on there is a black mass of rock rising from the surf, breakers pounding against it.

"It is my dream, Tom. It is the place I dreamed of."

"Those ponies have you bewitched."

"No. I remember it."

"It looks like a dozen places at home, Karen. You must have dreamed of one of those."

"Perhaps." But she does not believe him. Something is on the other side of that rock, she is thinking. Something is waiting there. But it is a nice thing.

The crow flies overhead, circles the black rock, and caws loudly. Karen hurries ahead. There is mustard growing in the field; the path is grassy. Crickets sing.

Before she gets to the rock Karen stops and waits for Tom. They go on together.

On the other side of the rock, standing in the sand looking up at them, is a small, dirty child. Karen nearly laughs. It is a little girl not more than six, bedraggled, muddy, but rosy underneath. Her hair is dark and straight; her eyes are dark and very bold.

"There was hardly time to wish," the child says. "Did you wish?"

"I made a wishing ring." Karen holds out her finger.

"Might do. Never heard of that."

"I'm sorry if we spoiled your wish."

"Oh, I made it all right. Had to hurry, though. Didn't see them till you started them up."

"Were they Sand Ponies?"

"Of course! You're new here!"

"And they're wild?"

"Yes. And magic."

"For everyone?"

"Not if you hurt 'em."

Tom is silent, listening.

"Where did you come from?" asks the child.

"From across the fields," says Karen. "And you?"

The child points silently. Karen and Tom see footprints making a long line in the wet sand to the base of the cliff. They look away to where she is pointing, but they see only a clump of trees, with hills beyond.

"What is your name?" asks Tom.

"Jana," says the child, scratching her knee. "Where are you going?"

"Nowhere much," says Tom.

"Are you running away?"

The children look startled. What has made her say this? Their canvas packs, perhaps.

"Would you tell if we were?" ventures Karen. Tom looks at her. This is a crazy thing to say.

"No, we won't tell," the child says. "You can come with us."

"Us?"

"There's more. There's Lisa. We're twins." The child turns, looking over her shoulder. Coming from a spot out of sight against the cliff is a second child, exactly like the first, and just as dirty. The crow screams loudly.

Now there are two muddy urchins. They put out two grubby hands. Karen takes Jana's, Tom, Lisa's. They start to walk down the beach.

"You don't live anywhere," says Lisa. It is not a question.

"Not now," Karen says. I must be bemused, she thinks. What's the matter with me?

"You will live with us," says Lisa matter-of-factly.

When they have skirted odd fields and crossed another stream and have walked through the fragrant twilight of a redwood grove and have waded a larger, deeper stream, there, in a field of tall grass, sits an ancient barn, silvered by the sea wind. It has no house, no fences—there is no sign of life at all.

A shaft of sunlight cuts across the open barn door, making a spider web glitter. A moment later, a spry, gray-haired person steps out into the sunlight wiping her hands on a ragged apron. A lop-eared hound comes out behind her, and the smell of ginger cookies floats out with her like a cloud. There is no house to hold a kitchen, but ginger cakes are cooking somewhere, and the crow has come to sit on the roof of the barn. A willow tree stands in the yard.

"Sarah, Sarah, Sarah." The little girls let go of hands and run madly ahead. "Sarah, look what we found!" they both shout.

There she stands in the sunlight, wiping her hands and watching the children come across the field, her blue eyes bright. There is Sarah Paddyfoot, and she looks like someone you might have known forever.

But let us go back a minute, before we go ahead.

It is a frosty, blue-hazed morning, early in the spring, about the time that Kippy began to yearn for home. The crow sits on a dead bush near the barn, watching for mice in the white stubble of the field. But something is amiss. There is something strange in the air, and he flies up toward heaven, where he can see the land below.

What is this? Across the field comes a figure, stepping starchily in the frozen grass. Across the fields she comes walking, gray hair a straggle, old brown skirt awry, old blue tennis shoes scrunching in the frozen stubble. Blue eyes sparkling, nose pink from the cold, she covers the fields with the stride of a girl, swinging her satchel and looking up at the crow, who caws at her, telling her she is trespassing.

"Hush, you crow!" says Sarah Paddyfoot. "I have come to stay. You'd better get used to me, sir! I haven't found a place yet, but I will, and you'd better treat me kindly!"

No one will ever know why Sarah Paddyfoot turned and crossed the fields to the old barn. Nothing could have been more unlikely, for someone wanting work. There were nice houses in the village farther north, and certainly she could see their roofs tucked among the hills, and the inviting whiffs of smoke from their chimneys. But across the fields to the barn she went.

One might go there to steal a little firewood, or to look for relics, or to offer charity if one saw a sign of life. Or one might go looking for a lost dog, or a stray cow. But to go there for a job? No, never.

But Sarah Paddyfoot came, moving jauntily across the fields, arguing with the crow. Jana and Lisa watched her come, two small faces peering from the loft of the barn. Bo watched her come, growling softly and wagging his tail. John watched her come, from where he was washing by the stream, and Mr. Tillman watched her come from where he was planing boards inside the barn.

There are four Tillmans—five, counting Bo—and every one watched Sarah Paddyfoot come across the fields and set her satchel down by the barn door and look around her, at the old barn, at the little pile of new lumber inside, at the Tillmans, and at old Bo and the crow.

She never went away again; a motherless house needs someone, and Sarah Paddyfoot had come to stay. One more plate for supper; one more bed in the barn.

And now, led home like stray calves, a grubby twin guiding each, come Karen and Tom.

Two more plates for supper; two more beds in the barn.

Sarah Paddyfoot gives them milk and ginger cakes

and sends the dirty twins to wash themselves. "To-gether, we call them J.L.," says Sarah Paddyfoot. "Separate, they are Jana and Lisa, but together they are J.L. Together," continues Sarah Paddyfoot, "they are something more than two little girls; something like a swarm. Or a plague." She pours more milk for the children.

CHAPTER

10

It is a tall barn, with a loft above, full height, and there is a proper stairway leading up, and a railing around the loft where it looks down into the barn below.

In five of the stalls below there are five cots made of hay, and in one huge stall, near the open barn door, where the ginger-cookie smell is heaviest, there is the skeleton of a kitchen: rough walls, little old stove standing alone, sink set into a cabinet of many colors as if it were put together from many bits and pieces—but well put together, Tom notices, straight and true. There are apple boxes for cupboards, but also a light frame of new lumber where someone has started to make cabinets, and this, too, is no amateur job. Tom looks questioningly at Sarah Paddyfoot, taking more cookies from the oven. "Not me," she says. "I'm no carpenter. Mr. Tillman did that."

THE SAND PONIES

The window is still just a square hole, but big, letting in the morning and a branch or two of the willow tree as well.

"John and Mr. Tillman are in town," says Sarah, "taking apart an old house for lumber and such.

Plumbing, too! Have us a real bathroom soon, good hot shower. Water pipes already in," she says, indicating the sink. "Could use some help, that man could," she says, looking at Tom. "John's mighty fine help, all right, learning real good, but the more hands the better, for this work." She lifts the last cookies off the tin and sets them to cool in a cupboard, closing the door securely and glancing out the window at the crow, who is sitting in the willow tree peering at her. "Old robber!" she mutters. "Come on, kids, you can pick out your rooms." She chuckles. "Have a bucket to wash in if you like, then come on with J.L. and me to get some clams for supper."

The shore can be seen from the barn door, white dunes sloping gently down to it, patches of tall russet grass making patterns in the wind. The beach itself is wide and wet, for the tide is out, and the clams, dug deep and fast or lost, are plentiful and good sized. In the distance a dark, heavy rain cloud lies over the sea. The sand is bare of footprints, save their own and the little forked ones of the shore birds. Bo goes to play in the water, frolicking like a pup, and far out beyond the breakers a seal watches them, watches Bo playing there. Gulls cry overhead, the surf pounds and foams, and the crow comes out of the sky to scold them.

"There is every kind of bird track," Karen says, "but no animal prints."

"You'll see animals one morning, see coon and pos-
sum," says Sarah Paddyfoot, plopping a big clam into
her bucket. "Be Sand Ponies looking in your window
one morning if you're good to them."

Karen looks startled, then laughs.

"Think not?" says Sarah Paddyfoot. "Wild they
are, but you put grain out, don't scare 'em, you'll see!"

"That's true," shouts Jana. "That's really true.
They come to the door at night, sometimes, look
right in. Only for the grain, though," she adds. "Must
be very still when they come. They're really fairy
ponies."

Sarah smiles.

"Where did they come from, Sarah?" Karen asks.

"Well, some say they are the ghosts of children
who would not leave the seashore," Sarah says, grinning. "Some say they're wards of the devil, sent to
plague us. Some think they're fairies," she says,
glancing at J.L. "That you can wish on them. Who
knows, for sure? Not I," she says with a twinkle in
her eye. "Were here when I came, here when the
Tillmans came before me. Be here when we're all
gone, dare say."

"It seems strange," Karen says, "that they could live
like that with so many people around. Folks must
catch a good many."

"Pretty strong feeling around here," Sarah says.
"Keeps them safe. People say, you hurt those ponies,
bother them, they'll bring the worst kind of luck.

Wouldn't want to try it. Hear some weird stories, that's sure."

"Then we know someone who will have bad luck, the more the better," Tom says.

"Who's that?" asks Jana, wide-eyed, imagining the suffering of some deserving soul.

As they settle down in the grass to rest, the clams covered with wet sacks to keep them cool, the children tell Sarah and J.L. about the strange ranch and the starving ponies, and about the man and woman from the Black Turtle. Sarah Paddyfoot looks thoughtful at this, but she says nothing and the children go on to tell about all that happened before that, and after, even about Karen's dream of the path by the sea and the black rock, and something waiting there. "That was us, waiting," says Lisa. "Us!"

"In a dream, imagine!" says Jana.

If you can come out of a dream, Karen thinks, why can't Kippy, too? She looks out across the rolling dunes and the blowing grass at the swelling sea, and she imagines the little horse coming across the sand toward her, ears up, black mane flying. Why can't Kippy, too?

When the horses lag Kippy drives them on. They all have bite marks on necks and withers and rumps. They don't kick back or nip any more; he is wild to travel faster. They are becoming a disciplined little band; they drive well and graze only when Kippy lets them. Tolly is growing slower as the days pass and needs to graze more than the others, but even she is beginning to sniff the air and dream of home.

They have not only to go north, but to cross the mountains and move west to the sea. They travel first in that direction, moving at night and laying up in the daytime, hidden by trees or boulders. Where Kippy has gotten his knowledge no one can say. Perhaps his wiliness comes from his mountain ancestors, or perhaps from need. He does well on little grass, far better than the other horses, who are growing thinner.

The mountain rocks are hard to climb, the grass sparse and too new to have much strength. Some snow still clings in high places. There are mountain lion here, and bear. Twice they smell the dreadful bear smell and panic, even Kippy, scattering down the mountain, terrified. But some sense draws them together again, and Kippy will not go on until all are worked into a bunch once more.

They travel many weeks, and Tolly is having a harder time of it. She grows slow and irritable, and she starts to resist Kippy. She is now heavy with foal, and she is not getting enough to eat. But Kippy drives her on.

Then one morning as the sun rises they stand on the edge of a steep hill—they have been carefully descending for hours—and gaze at a stretch of flat country dotted with oak trees and pine and carpeted with grass.

They have crossed the coast range. Lean and tired, they look before them, then hurry down into the plain.

For many days they stay here. There is water, and the grass is tall and mature.

Soon they begin to grow fatter, and as they do they start to lift their heads once more and to gaze eagerly toward home.

Even Tolly becomes anxious to go on. She, too, is beginning to know the obsession that has driven Kippy; her colt will be born at home, where the grass is sweetest. Now it is she who starts first in the evening, it is she who is impatient. Between them, she and Kippy herd the little band, though not much herding is needed now, only directing. Kippy always seems to know which way is safest.

There are still foothills to cross, but the winter rain has made strong pasture, the grazing is easy, and the traveling is fast. Some days later they have left the foothills and are working their way between farm fences, down dirt roads—always at night—avoiding the barking dogs. Now Kippy walks out, head swinging. He can smell the sea.

CHAPTER

11

In front of the old barn, under the willow tree, the table is set for supper. There is clam chowder, bisquits, and berry pie. Karen is washed and so is Tom. Even the twins are clean, two scrubbed little girls.

"There will be a brick terrace," says Mr. Tillman, "here under the tree, and glass doors where the barn doors are. Over there will be a low brick wall." He is tall and tanned and solid-looking. His brown hair is cut close and his eyes are very blue. John has dark hair and eyes, like the twins. He is perhaps a year older than Tom, but no taller.

"It will be lovely," Karen says, seeing the old barn as Mr. Tillman sees it.

It is a well-made barn. The ceiling towers high above the loft, the rafters sweep away under a good roof. As Mr. Tillman and John talk the old gray

walls begin to sprout windows, the windows grow verandas, the stalls become rooms, and the center part of the barn turns itself into a living room with bookshelves and a fireplace at one end.

"It took some looking," says Mr. Tillman, "to find the place we wanted." He leans comfortably back in his chair and lights his pipe. Lisa blows out the match and Jana makes a rude noise at her. Mr. Tillman frowns and J.L. settle down once more.

"When Mama died," Jana says, "we did not want to stay in the city. We came here. We sold our house and came here. Papa said we were too much for the city."

"I am a carpenter," Mr. Tillman continues. "I can make as good a living here, with the village close, as I can in the city, and have time to myself, too. The city's no place for children. Not these children, anyway. Jana's right, they overflow into trouble there." He pauses and draws deeply, and Karen thinks how nice a pipe smells, mixed with the sea air. "And what about you two? Is the city not your kind of place either, then?"

"No, I guess it's not," Tom says. He doesn't say any more, and Mr. Tillman doesn't ask.

"I could use some strong help," he says finally, looking at Tom, "if you were planning to stay in this part of the country for a while."

"We did want to work," Tom says. "We were

going to get jobs somewhere. Could we really be useful? How can you be sure?"

"Suppose I give you a week to try," Mr. Tillman says. "If you're a good carpenter, you'll get room and board. If not," he knocks his pipe into an empty nail can, "you can go to work in the village and board with us, if you care to stay."

But what will I do? Karen thinks. I want to work, too. I can drive a nail as well as Tom can.

Mr. Tillman is looking at her. "With two extra pairs of hands," he says, "we should be pretty snug by fall." He doesn't mention school.

Later, as Tom is helping Karen make her straw bed in one of the stalls, Karen says, "We'll have to tell Mr. Tillman we ran away. We can't stay without telling him."

"I know," Tom says. "Then perhaps he won't want us."

"Do you think he'll make us go away?"

"No," Tom says, "I don't."

"Neither do I," says Karen. "But what if we get him in trouble?"

"Well, he must be told, then decide for himself if he wants to take the chance," Tom says. "If he wants us to leave, we will."

"Yes," Karen says. "Good night."

"Good night," says Tom, leaving her door ajar. They both know Tom is the one to tell Mr. Tillman— it doesn't need discussing.

"Wait, Tom," Karen calls after him. "What about the Black Turtle people? What shall we do about them?"

"Wait until I talk to Mr. Tillman, Karen. Maybe he will know something."

"All right. Good night, Tom."

"Good night."

CHAPTER

12

At the first break of day the crow screams. There is a badger in the chicken run, and he doesn't want it there. There are no chickens, and the crow wouldn't care if there were, but he doesn't want the badger in the chicken run.

Sarah Paddyfoot sits up in bed and looks out her window at the sky, just turning light, the moon still hanging there palely. We must get some chickens soon, thinks Sarah, give the old crow something to yell about. He might as well be of some use. He probably won't yell then. Let the badger get all the chickens. Hmph. She gets out of bed and begins to think about breakfast. With such a racket, everyone will be up soon as you can say Scat.

She dips into the bucket of cold water standing on her orange-crate table, and has a good scrub.

Soon she is dressed and into the kitchen, muttering, "Blackberry jam; bisquits and blackberry jam; scrambled eggs. Wish we had some chickens. Must get that run fixed up. Free food, chickens are. No harm in that. Lord gave us chickens to feed us. Might as well use 'em!"

"Taking the Lord's name in vain, Sarah?" asks Mr. Tillman, coming into the kitchen.

"Nothing of the kind," says Sarah. "Said the Lord gave us chickens to feed us. Might as well use 'em."

Glancing out the door at the still screaming crow,

Mr. Tillman guesses who started this. "Not a bad idea, though," he thinks aloud. "Got us a young lady to care for them now. S'pose she's any good with chickens?"

"Sure I am," says Karen, coming in. "I can take care of chickens. We're not city children," she says, preparing the way for Tom, who stands in the door behind her.

"No, sir, we're not," Tom says, "and I want to talk to you about that." Tom waits. Mr. Tillman fills his coffee cup, looks at Tom, then goes out into the yard.

"Running away?" Mr. Tillman helps him.

"Yessir."

"From your folks?"

"Oh, no, sir. Aunt and uncle."

"Parents dead?"

"Yes, sir," Tom says. "It was an uncle and aunt we were sent to live with. They're the only relatives we have. I guess the next thing would have been a home."

"What did they do?" asks Mr. Tillman. "Some reason you left, that's sure."

Tom looks grateful. "Drank," he says. "Really drank, Mr. Tillman. For days."

"I see," says Mr. Tillman, lighting his pipe. "Will they look for you?"

"I don't think so," Tom says, and tells him about the note.

"Good thinking. Doesn't look like there's much to worry about now. Face school when we come to it. Think of something."

"Then you don't want us to leave?" Tom asks.

"Not on your life!" says Mr. Tillman. "Lose two good hands?" He grins at Tom, and bends to light his pipe.

"And there's something else, sir," continues Tom. "We came up the road from the south."

"Yes?"

"Well, we stopped at a big ranch to ask for a job. Big white house and barn."

"I know the place."

"Do you know anything about it?"

"No, only where it is." He looks questioningly at Tom.

"Well, there wasn't a soul around when we got there. There were crops growing, all right, but no stock. We went back to the barn to look, thinking the people would return soon. We went in, and the barn was deserted, too, we thought, but then . . ." And Tom tells Mr. Tillman about the Sand Ponies, and about the strange behavior of the men.

"What do you think?" he asks when he is finished. "Do you think it was something illegal? Or were we just imagining it?"

Mr. Tillman draws on his pipe, gazing at the sea. "It does sound mighty funny," he says finally. "One thing sure, the sheriff's a good sort. Won't hurt to tell him. If nothing's wrong, no harm done. If something is, he'll find out what."

"But what about us? Won't he wonder where we came from?"

"I don't need to tell him anything about you two. He knows me. If I say I heard this, but can't tell him where it came from, he won't ask, Tom. He's an honorable man." He gets up, putting his hand lightly on Tom's shoulder. "Smells like breakfast's ready. Don't you worry, Son. I'll see that it's all right. But I won't tell him if you don't want me to."

Tom hesitates. "Yes, tell him. I wouldn't feel right, not." They go toward the willow tree, where Sarah is calling breakfast.

"It's all right," says Mr. Tillman, smiling at Karen. "Get us some chickens, you'll have yourself part of a job, anyhow."

Karen grins.

"Egg chickens or eating chickens?" shouts Jana, climbing down out of the tree.

"Some of both, I guess," says Mr. Tillman.

"Roasting chickens! And a turkey!" she says.

"You won't want a turkey," John says, laughing. "Mean. Chase you all over the yard."

"Wouldn't dare!" says Jana.

"Oh, wouldn't he?" John laughs and reaches up into the tree to grab a dangling foot. "Come on, Lisa, breakfast's down here." The feet come down, attached to a child, and they all find places at the table, the twins set securely at either side of their father.

"We'll have to fix the chicken run," John says, buttering a bisquit. "Needs new wire, and new lumber, too, in spots."

"I can do that," Karen offers, "with maybe some help putting on the wire."

"I can hold the wire if you can hammer," says Sarah Paddyfoot.

"I can hammer," says Karen.

After breakfast, as Karen enters the barn, the sunlight is spilling through the back door, making the sawhorses and lumber look golden. For a minute she stands looking about her, and tries to imagine how the living room will look with windows where the door is, sun streaming in onto rugs and couch where sawhorses and tools now sit, the fireplace rising at the end, flanked by bookshelves. She begins to think about colors for the room, perhaps gold, the shade of the new wood, with a bit of orange the color of the nail boxes, a bit of blue the color of the sky.

Quite lost in planning it, she stands for a long time, dreaming. Only yesterday, she thinks, we were cold and hiding and had no home at all. And before that, it was worse. I hope we can stay here. I hope nothing happens to make us go back again.

The boys and Mr. Tillman are hard at work, and finally Karen picks up hammer and nails, scraps of board, and a handsaw, and goes to her own job, humming. From the kitchen comes a clatter as Sarah Paddyfoot washes dishes. In the willow tree the crow caws loudly, and old Bo pads out to growl softly at him.

So the children settle into the old barn, and soon it seems as if they have always been there. Sea breezes blow, grass ripples, plovers and sandpipers call; meadowlarks sing, gulls cry, and the crow watches and scolds.

Grain is put at the door every night, but the Sand Ponies do not come. "They know there is someone new," says Mr. Tillman. "It will take a while. Meantime, that crow makes a pig of himself."

Walls get built, windows cut, the bathroom is usable and nearly ready for paint. Berries are picked, clams dug, fish caught, cattails and other wild food gathered; wild onions and garlic perfume the kitchen. Now the barn is part barn, part house; part old silvered wood and part new lumber. It settles into a symphony of hammer rhythm, saws singing through board, gull cries, the voices of boys and the man, the laughter and quarreling of the twins. And always there is the raucous voice of the crow, the twins shouting back at him.

When the crow steals Jana's locket the morning is shattered with caws and angry cries.

Jana, in order to try a swim in the old horse trough, has taken off all her clothes, and her precious locket as well, laying it on top. Lisa would have followed her, but she is away with Karen and Sarah Paddyfoot, picking berries.

Down the crow swoops, lighting on top of Jana's clothes and cocking his head. The locket shines brightly. When Jana sees him she shouts, but it is too late. He leaps into the air, the locket dangling from his polished beak.

Jana climbs from the trough and grabs a stone to throw just as John comes around the corner of the barn. He grabs the rock, Jana's hand still around it. "What are you doing?"

"He has my locket," wails Jana.

"Well, what did you take it off for?" asks John, frowning at the dripping little girl.

"To swim."

"So I see! But you can't throw a rock at him! He doesn't know it's wrong. You shouldn't have left it, Jana."

"I can too throw a rock," shouts Jana, jerking away and raising her arm.

"Well, you can, but you won't hit him," says John, stepping back.

"I will, too!"

"Besides, he's in his own place. It's not your sky!"

"Not his either!"

"More his than yours!"

"It's not! It's God's sky. And my locket!"

"And God's bird, Jana!"

THE SAND PONIES

"If God made that old crow, he didn't mean for him to steal my locket!"

"All the same, God's sky, and God's bird, too," says John, going into the house and leaving Jana to her own devices.

Lisa has returned, and comes up behind Jana, quiet for once. She still has her own locket. Jana eyes it. Lisa goes quickly into the house, following John.

The crow sits in the willow tree for a long while, then flies to a tall pine, hiding the locket securely in his nest.

Jana glares. It is a very tall tree.

CHAPTER

13

No one loses five horses, with snow and plenty of mud to show their tracks, without going after them. It is among the rocky cliffs that the trail finally vanishes, and Mr. Elber must go home. He does all the proper things, notifying the ranchers along the way, the rangers, and the police. He knows why horses leave their pastures in the springtime when they are far from home, and he calls Portland, saying, "Watch for them in a couple of months. They should be there by then—if they make it."

All along the way men are alerted to the passing of the horses, and riders watch the hills as they go about their work. And all along the way the horses, blessed with some impossible luck, travel under the noses of those who search for them.

THE SAND PONIES

On a low hill, hidden by bracken and flowering bushes, the tramp sits, watching the great white barn and the ranch house, watching the roads that lead to them. He is eating beans from a can and drinking coffee, while over a tiny fire, green cattails are boiling. He has watched the barn for many weeks, moving off across the country sometimes, then coming back to it.

The ranch has been quiet since yesterday evening, when the red truck pulled into the barn, then left a few minutes later. There has been shouting once or twice, faintly heard, and this morning, before it was light, the tramp made his way down to the barn, looked into the deserted, muddied stalls and the feed room, and poked about here and there, returning to the hill just in time to avoid being chased away, or worse.

The cattails smell good, and when they are done he picks one up, blows on it, and chews on it like an ear of corn. I wonder how they knew all that, he thinks, remembering the children. He has not had the nerve to try cooked flowers, but he may. He may. He's glad the crow has not returned this time; he is such a noisy bird.

"It's so lovely here, I can't believe it's real," Karen says one evening as she and Tom walk barefoot along the edge of the surf, watching the sun go down. "And yet it seems as if we have always been here, as if we

have known the Tillmans and Sarah Paddyfoot forever. And Bo, too," she says as the hound shakes a
spray of ocean over them.

"Too good to be real," Tom says. "Do you think it
is only one of your dreams, after all?"

"I hope not. What will we do when school starts,
Tom? It frightens me to think of it."

"Mr. Tillman said he'd figure out something, and
somehow, I'm sure he will. I don't know," he continues, "he makes me feel as if he could take care of
anything. Even school. I must talk to him about it,
though. He says"—Tom pauses to pick up a shell—
"he says my carpentry is as good as John's, that you

and I have been a good bit of help." He hands the shell to Karen and watches Bo leap into the surf. "We'll think of something, before school starts," he promises.

After many weeks Kippy and his band come down the last valley, cross the last field, and stand gazing at the sea. Kippy looks for a long time, then lies down and rolls. He gets up snorting and begins to play; he chases the pony, then bucks off toward the beach, shying back when he reaches the sand and returning to graze with the others.

They begin to move up the coast, having many times to go back and around fenced pastures, or out onto the beach at night when they cannot be seen. There is plenty of grazing, the going is good, and they should make good time, but Tolly is growing very slow, holding them back. Some days she is eager to move ahead, and will swing heavily along beside Kippy for a while; more often she will not move at all, but puts back her ears and will not tolerate Kippy's nipping. But Kippy does not nip so hard; he is growing more careful. This is strange; he does not want to badger her as before. There is something different about her. What is it, Kippy? You are only a small, ornery gelding—What do you know about colts? Nevertheless, he is tender with her, and lets her set the pace, choosing whether to travel or to loaf along and graze. At least he is by the sea, and the meadows are green.

In a small apartment in San Francisco a redheaded young lady sits at a card table before the fire eating her dinner. She is small and fine-boned, with a golden hue to her skin. On the card table, besides an omelet and a salad, a cup of coffee and a half-eaten roll, is a pile of books, a map, and an untidy stack of letters. On the couch, facing her, sits her yellow cat, Abbey, watching her.

"I will teach," says Mary McCamley, "in the smallest village there is, where all the children come to one room, and help each other learn; a place where the sea roars and the sun shines and the storms are the wildest storms you've ever seen, Abbey!" She puts down her coffee cup and looks across at the cat intently, as if waiting for an answer. Abbey blinks. "We will have a cottage there," Mary McCamley continues, "for the two of us, Abbey." She pauses, then pours herself more coffee. Abbey blinks again, and yawns.

One morning Kippy raises his head and puts up his ears. There is movement on the hill across the stream, and as he watches he sees a herd of ponies slipping through the scrub trees and the tall grass on the hill, silent as cats. It is very early; they are coming to drink. No tame horses, these, Kippy knows. They move differently. They are alert, wary.

There is a great band of them. Mostly roans and grays they are, sand-colored, half hidden in the browning grass. They are hardy little things, no bigger than Kippy. The leader has seen Kippy and pauses. The wind is the wrong way and he can't smell if there is man near, but these are strange horses. His ears are back; he turns, and the other ponies, obedient and wary, turn with him. Soon they are gone.

Across the mountains Mr. Elber has had a message. "We're not sure, yet," says the sheriff. "We have some wild horses here, and it could be them, but one of the farmers swears he's seen some big horses, bigger than these wild ponies." He pauses. "What's that? Sure! Sure I will, first thing I know any more. I'd like to catch the whole bunch of wild ones, too, while I'm at it. What's that? Oh, yes, whole flock of 'em. Cute little things, but a bother, running loose—folks here think they bring luck, or some such thing. Trample a lot of gardens, those ponies do. What's that? Yessir, we'll catch those critters if they're yours, all right. Let you know right away."

Mary McCamley, still in pajamas, sets down her orange-juice glass and reads the letter again. What teacher would leave a lovely small town by the sea? Well, some teacher had, had gotten married, or retired. Or just moved away. Someone had. "And lucky for us, Abbey!" says Mary McCamley. "About time, I'd say! Summer's wasting, here in the city!"

Later, jeep half loaded, apartment torn apart, Mary McCamley stands in the middle of the packing. "There really isn't much, don't have much to pack. Sure takes room though, little as it is! Wonder if we'll get it all in, Abbey." Abbey blinks. "You all packed, Abbey? Catnip mice and everything? Won't take me long, you know, even with this mess! What's that you say? Real mice there? I wouldn't be surprised!

"Just think, Abbey, a one-room schoolhouse and all! Come on, Abbey, get a move on—summer's wasting, sitting here!"

When the old tramp leaves the hill above the ranch, he has been back to the barn again, at night, and he carries away more than he brought. He makes his way along the hills, past the ranch, then down to the road where the walking is easier. He passes the farm where Tom and Karen hid, but it is not light yet, and the dog does not bark, for he is asleep in the house, his head on Jerry's pillow. In the corral a sleek pony moves warily away, watching. The tramp stares at him. He has heard of Sand Ponies and thinks this is one of them. He looks healthy enough; maybe someone has made a pet of him.

He goes on his way, watching the sun rise just as

Karen and Tom did. On a hill near the sea he sees dark shapes moving, and he watches them. Must be the Sand Ponies, he thinks. Mighty few of them though, half a dozen, maybe. By the time the sun is well up he is hungry, and he pauses by the road to eat and to drink from the stream; then he heads on toward the village, whose roofs he can see in the distance, tucked among the hills.

At the Black Turtle, morning customers are getting breakfast at the dark bar; special customers, wiping their breakfasts from their chins and tucking little packages in their pockets as they get into cars and drive away.

At the ranch the three men have worked all night, and the woman, too. She has gone off to the inn, and the men want their rest. "One more thing before you knock off," Charley says. "Early yet—we'll get out and get those traps set. Get that truck in here, Tip."

"Aw, for ———, Charley, not this morning. What the devil's the matter with you?"

Charley grabs the man, pulling his collar and choking him. "I said *now!* Get out to that truck, Tip, get moving!"

"Kay wouldn't like it," says Ed.

"You tell her, and see what you get."

"Okay, Charley, I'm coming."

"Get those ropes out of the bin. Come on, get a move on!"

Soon they are in the truck and moving across a little back road between the hills.

Sarah Paddyfoot stands knee-deep in a patch of bright orange day lilies, gazing about her with a little sigh. She looks up, hoping that not even the crow will disturb her this morning.

The meadow is no bigger than a good-sized yard, surrounded by hillocks and trees, so that it is sheltered from passing eyes. The lilies are thick as garden flowers. Sarah leans down and begins to dig the bulbs, putting the long-stemmed blooms in a basket. Quickly she works, humming a little, finally sitting down among the lilies so that only the top of her head, like a great white moth, can be seen above the flowers. The day is still, and butterflies come to hover over her. The sea murmurs to itself, and the crickets hum. The crow does not appear, and all is peaceful. No one watches her.

No one. No one but the old tramp, standing silently at the edge of the woods, blending with the trees. He stands for a long time, smiling a little. Another lily-gatherer!

Sarah hums softly. Finally, looking up to brush away a gnat, she sees the tramp. She sits quite still, looking at him.

"Are they good to eat raw, or only cooked?" he asks her.

"Both," she says. "How long have you been standing there spying on me?"

He laughs. "Not long. Was drinking at the stream. Heard a rustle, thought it was a bear."

"Bear! Ha! Do I look like a bear? Bear in the lily bed!"

"Well, Sand Pony, maybe."

"Ah. Could be that. But it's not. It's just me, old lady in rags."

This is an exaggeration, but he lets it pass. "Well, how do you eat them raw? Salad? I've seen them cooked, but never tasted either."

"Perhaps you'll come to dinner and find out."

"But you don't know me. I might be a tramp."

"Thought you were!" says Sarah. "Look like one!"

"So I do. Well. And so I am."

"We eat 'bout six o'clock. That's on account of the twins get hungry so early."

"Yours?"

"No, more's the blessing. Family I work for."

"Won't they mind!"

"Mind? Be delighted."

"The missus won't care?"

"No missus. Just a father. Young man. Needs a wife. Kids no good without a mother. I can handle 'em though, till something better comes along. Come now, let me show you where. Six o'clock sharp, you remember."

"Yes, ma'am," he says, stepping out of the grove and going with Sarah to where he can see the barn in the distance. "Six o'clock sharp." He leaves her, thanking her again and melting away into the grove.

"Hmph," says Sarah Paddyfoot. "Bears indeed! Never heard a tramp speak that well before; nice fellow. Feed him day lilies, I will."

CHAPTER

14

On the cliff by the ocean Karen is leaning against a twisted tree, chewing a blade of grass and gazing at the breakers. She is halfway to the village with saw blades to be sharpened, and an order for baby chicks and for feed. There is a grocery list in the rope bag she carries, and measurements of windows for the glazier.

The day is foggy and cool. Bo rushes in and out of the waves, and the twins are far ahead, racing through grass as tall as they are. Above, the crow keeps pace, screaming. Karen smiles. Ahead is a small grove of pines, and beyond that she can see the roofs of the village, surrounded by low hills. As she nears the trees and begins to turn away from the sea she calls to Bo.

The twins run through the grass like hidden ani-

mals and tear into the pine grove, shouting. There is
a loud crash ahead of them, and the little girls stop
perfectly still, staring, big-eyed, as the Sand Ponies
leap through the grove away from them and out into
the meadow, running hard.

The twins are silent as they watch the last running
ponies, hear the last sounds of crashing in the grove.

Karen, too, is still. She is making a wish.

THE SAND PONIES

Quickly, wishes made, the children hurry through the grove. The ponies are far away, crossing the hills, still running. No one says a word. They join hands and go on toward the village, slowly, gazing still at the hills.

The hardware store is dim and smells of strange, exotic things. The twins disappear like elves, to touch and smell in silent delight, as Karen hands over the saw blades in their little envelopes.

The proprietor is a grizzled, sour-looking old man, but with a twinkle hidden somewhere underneath. "Spook'll getcha back there," he says to the twins as they disappear into the storeroom, where most customers do not go.

"Not us!" shouts Lisa. "We're magic! We've wished, this morning!"

There is a loud screaming of the grinder as the old man starts to sharpen the blades. "Saw the Sand Ponies, didja?" he asks of Karen as he stops for a minute. "You make a wish, too?"

"Oh, yes!" She hopes he will not ask what. "It puzzles me, how they can run free where so many people live. Are they really magic?" she asks, smiling at him.

"Likely," he says shortly, starting on another blade; then, "Devils, some say." He goes on with the grinding.

Then later, "Devils. Curse on 'em, some say! You feed 'em, good luck, but harm those ponies, that's the

end of luck for you, girl. Happened more than once.
Old man Greeb, he lost his whole flock, nine hundred
sheep, he lost. Got the sickness. Shot a Sand Pony,
fed it to his dogs. Lost 'em all, all nine hundred."
He turns to finish the blades, leaving Karen to pet
Bo and wonder.

"Another time," he continues, finished with the
blades, "man came down from the city, brought
trucks, said those were wild ponies and no season on
'em, was gonna catch 'em up and sell 'em, no one
could stop him, all legal, he said. Well, legal it may
have been, but catch 'em, he didn't. Ran right over
him, the whole great stampeding bunch of 'em, right
down in Middle Canyon, there. Folks around here,
they let those ponies alone. Less it's to feed 'em in
the winter. Brings good luck, that does. Larry Crail,
he had twins and a record litter of hogs and a whole
full dozen good speckled pointers, all in one year.
And cleared a cool twenty thousand, besides," he
adds. "Fed 'em all winter, Larry did." He spits onto
the sawdust floor and turns to make Karen's change,
giving her a bill and putting the blades back into
their envelopes. "Get your wish, likely," he says.
"You don't look a mean one to me, miss!"

She gives him the order for glass, for feed and a
batch of chicks—"Need a brooder for 'em now, de-
liver 'em in a couple of weeks, be all right," he says—
collects the twins, and goes out into the street.

The village is small, huddled together comfortably

at the base of the hills, its streets crooked and its roofs climbing between the hills on one side and dropping down to a meadow on the other. There is a stream running through town, and Karen wonders if the Sand Ponies ever come here to drink. She guesses not.

"There's the schoolhouse," says Lisa as they pass a small white box of a building with a bell on the top. "We'll go there this year," she says, "but we can already read. First grade's for babies!" Karen laughs at her.

Karen looks up. Someone is looking at her, staring. He is a white-bearded man, with very blue eyes. A tramp? He looks like one. He goes on by, and she turns to watch as he makes his way down the street and around the corner, out of sight. Hmm, wonder what he was staring for, Karen thinks, then puts him out of her mind as the grocery appears before her. She digs for the list and goes in.

Mary McCamley looks too slight, too city-bred, to be driving her old brown jeep down the village street, too neat and lady-like. Abbey sits on the back of the seat with a paw on Mary's shoulder, purring and looking around as if she likes what she sees of the village.

"There is the schoolhouse," says Mary, stopping the jeep in a cloud of dust. She sits there for a minute, looking; then she climbs out of the jeep and goes up the steps to peer in the window. She tries the door. It is locked, of course, but through the window Mary can see the blackboard, rows of desks, the teacher's desk in front—my desk, thinks Mary—chalk still in the holder, big old dictionary on a table near the window, coat rack, all the usual things, the comfortable things. Mary smiles. She is holding Abbey, whose tail suddenly twitches, making Mary look around.

"School's not open, not till fall."

"No summer school?" says Mary, knowing there is not. She faces a grubby little girl not more than six, escorted by a big hound who seems to be smiling at Abbey.

"Oh, no! Never have school in the summer," says the child. "Weather's too nice for that! Come fall, though, bell'l ring, teacher'll come—new teacher, we're getting—then we'll read Shakespeare!"

Mouth open, eyes wide, Mary stares for a minute. Shakespeare, indeed! "Can you read?" she asks the child, putting Abbey down to nose at the dog as she seems determined to do.

"Of course we can! Read the newspaper. Come fall, read Shakespeare!" the child repeats.

"We?" Mary says, looking around.

"Twins," the child says shortly. "In the grocery. Here she comes."

From the door of the small country market comes a whole passel of children, varying somewhat as to size and degree of dirtiness. There is no difficulty in recognizing the other part of 'we' . . . The spit 'n' image, thinks Mary McCamley. Wonder if she plans on Shakespeare, too!

The second twin is eating a licorice, and holds another out to her sister. She extends a third to Mary, shyly, and Mary takes it, smiling.

Then everyone is quiet, staring. Some are petting the cat.

The children look at the jeep, at Abbey, at Mary more closely; then two go to peer inside the jeep. There is luggage there, and boxes of books. There is a world globe and a songbook.

The children stare again; then one says, "You're the new teacher! You're very early, though."

Mary smiles. "Yes. Well, do you mind?"

"You'll not start school yet?"

"Oh, no. Just want to get settled and wade in the ocean first."

This sounds sensible to the children, and they begin an alluring discussion of where Mary McCamley is to stay.

"Hotel," says one. "Last teacher stayed there."

"Too old," says another. "Food's no good. My pop says so."

"I'd like a small cottage near the beach," cuts in Mary, wondering if anyone will take her suggestion.

"Of course," says one big girl. "That would be best.

But where? Everything is taken, summertime. City folk," she says, not kindly. "Come school, you'll have no trouble, but now, everything's full!"

"Hmmm," says Mary McCamley. "Well, I will stay in the hotel until then, that's all."

"You won't like it," says one darkly.

"Pitch a tent," says another, delighted with the idea.

"That's a thought," says Mary, weighing the possibility of frowning city fathers and no job after all.

"Won't take your cat, the hotel," says a third.

"Oh, dear," says Mary.

"We will," says Lisa. The twins have been very quiet, listening, and watching Bo to see he doesn't get scratched.

"We will keep you and your cat," Jana pipes. "For the summer. Sleep on hay, you must. Or maybe get a cot, could do that, I guess." They grab each other suddenly and do a wild, circular dance in and out among the other children. "Real live teacher, right at home," shrieks Jana. Mary McCamley looks alarmed.

"Teach us Shakespeare," shouts Lisa. Mary looks helplessly about her, but all the children seem delighted with the idea. What is she to do?

Well, first things first, and she untangles herself and Abbey from the children and prepares to make her duty calls to the school board and such. She puts

Abbey safely in a large cage in the jeep, straightens her hair, and dusts off her shoes. The twins watch silently, and then Lisa steps up and begins to give directions. Her brown eyes are bold, but steady. Her directions are careful, with a ring of authority. "But what will your family say," asks Mary McCamley, "if I come barging in?"

"Papa will be very pleased," says Lisa. "So will all of us, specially Sarah Paddyfoot. You'll see!"

"Well, all right," says Mary, smiling.

It is at the jailhouse that Mary McCamley must present herself. How funny, she thinks. Oh, well. She goes up the steps, sensibly leaving Abbey in the car. There is a small waiting room with no one there to ask anything of, but through a door she can see part of a desk, some large feet propped up on it, and there is the smell of cigar smoke.

Knocking at the half-open door, Mary peers in. Three men sit there, one with his feet on the desk, two lounging comfortably. There is a great struggle to arise as she appears before them. She protests, but, no, finally, their coffee nearly spilled, they are all up and smiling at her. One, who seems in charge, must be the sheriff. The bearded one seems shy, perhaps ashamed of his ragged clothes. The other man, wearing Levi's and boots, makes himself ready to leave.

A long time later, with arrangements made to meet the school board and the proper papers to sign, coffeed, informed, and quite assured about the Till-mans, Mary takes her leave.

Outside, most of the children who had been at the schoolhouse are gathered around Mary's jeep, deep in loud argument.

Jana is shouting, her dark eyes angry, "Not either! Didn't come from Hell, no such thing! You don't know anything, Billy Greeb."

"Do, too," the little boy shouts back, his face close to Jana's. "Came from Hell. Devil sent 'em!"

Lisa, until then watching silently, looks hard at Billy, then turns on her sister, shouting, "Came from Hell on a dark, stormy night, all right. I saw 'em! Came to devil *you!*"

This is too much for Jana, and she grabs her sister's hair. There is a moment of turmoil until Karen has them separated. Mary McCamley stands discreetly by, not interfering.

"What on earth?" she asks Karen when there is a moment's silence. "Came from Hell on a dark night? What are they talking about?"

"The Sand Ponies," offers an older boy, stepping up. "Wild ones. They're just wild ponies. People think they . . ."

At that moment Jana breaks in, nearly crying with indignation. "Sand *Fairies!*" she says. "They're good, not devils! They make *my* wishes come true—that's cause I can talk to them!" This is not true, but she feels enough better, having said it, to allow herself to be guided toward the jeep by Karen, and climbs into the back seat next to Abbey's cage, where she will speak to no one but Abbey all the way home.

By the time they reach home she feels even better, for Lisa has apologized, fearing some dark retribution from the ponies if she does not, and it is understood, grudgingly, that she didn't mean it. "Fairies," she says, "I know that. I just felt sorry for Billy!" This is a lie, but it is ignored.

J. L. scramble out of the jeep together, shouting their news of Mary to Sarah Paddyfoot.

One more plate for supper and one more bed in the barn.

CHAPTER

15

Under the willow tree the table is laid with a yellow cloth, and there is a bouquet of day lilies in the center. A clam pie waits on top the oven, bubbling hot, and there is a salad of wild greens. Day-lily bulbs are simmering, and day-lily buds wait to be battered and fried. "My goodness, Sarah, where did you find them? I haven't seen a one close by!" Karen says. "You've been busy while we were away."

Sarah grins. "Oh, secret spot for day lilies. Take you there one day. I must have a few secrets, child! No, one more plate, places for nine."

"Well, Miss McCamley, yes. That's eight," says Karen, counting.

"Set for nine."

"Who else?"

"Oh, friend of mine. Met him in the day-lily patch."

"Why, Sarah! But who?"

"Don't rightly know. Tramp, maybe. Nice, though."

Karen is staring at Sarah. "Why, Sarah Paddyfoot, what have you been up to? A tramp, did you say? Did he have a white beard, and very blue eyes?"

"Friend of yours, too?" asks Sarah.

"Well, no, but I saw him in town. He sure did stare at me." She goes out with the plates, wondering. A tramp. Could he be the man in the cave, walking through the country? What had Sarah done, asking him here? Well, no sense in fussing. They'd find out soon enough. Too soon, maybe.

She can see Miss McCamley looking out the big loft window with Mr. Tillman and the boys. Abbey sits on her shoulder, tail twitching.

Will she stay? Karen wonders. It would be nice, nice to have her here.

When she looks again they have disappeared, but soon she hears pounding start in the barn, and she goes to see. In the stall next to her own Tom and John and Mr. Tillman are putting together a wood frame for Mary's straw bed. Karen smiles. "You'll stay, then?" she asks.

"Of course," says Mary McCamley, "though I could build my own bed." She is setting orange crates against the wall for shelves, and on these are her globe and her songbook, and next to them, Abbey, sitting very straight, watching it all.

When the bed is finished the boys scramble to get straw for it, startling Abbey into leaping from the box into the bedframe, where a moment later she is covered with straw and comes out mad, switching her tail. "Be careful, John!" Mr. Tillman frowns. Karen looks at him. She has not seen him cross before. But then he smiles. "Abbey, you must be quick in this house! Quick and nimble!"

Mary McCamley laughs at him as he sets Abbey back on the orange crate. "Have you spoiling her, that

THE SAND PONIES

cat will," she tells him. "I've known her a long time, takes advantage, she does, every chance she gets!"

Mr. Tillman laughs.

In the yard, beneath the tree, Sarah Paddyfoot straightens the day-lily vase. "To look at, these are," she says, and beside the tree, in a tilted chair, sits the tramp, blue eyes bright and face and clothes very clean for someone who has been walking over the country.

There are introductions all around, and the tramp, whose name is Roland, bows gallantly to the twins, making them giggle. Then, taking Mary's hand, he says, "Why, it's the teacher from the village. How nice to see you again!"

Mr. Tillman goes to the kitchen and comes back with a bottle of amber wine, Sarah Paddyfoot rises to bring the pie on, and soon all are seated, the two guests placed where they can see the red sun descending into the ocean. The crow, very interested, comes down onto a branch to look, but Sarah chases him away. Bo wags mournfully, but has his own plate, and Abbey, on a box, has hers.

"I will make a toast, then," says Roland, raising his glass.

" 'Shield my soul from its peril, due
For the sins I sinned my lifetime through.' "

Mary McCamley laughs gently, her glass half raised, then speaks softly:

THE SAND PONIES

" 'My friend, my Roland, God guard thy soul!
Never on earth such knight hath been,
Fields of battle to fight and win.
My pride and glory, alas, are gone!' "

"What is it, Papa? Is it Shakespeare?" The twins
pull at their father's sleeve, staring wide-eyed at
Roland and Miss McCamley.

Jack Tillman smiles. "It is 'The Song of Roland,' "
he says. "Listen.

And he smote, with passion uncontrolled,
On the heathen's helm, with its jeweled crown—
Through head, and cuirass, and body down,
And the saddle embossed with gold, till sank
The griding steel in the charger's flank;
Blame or praise him, the twain he slew.
'A fearful stroke!' said the heathen crew.
'I shall never love you,' Count Roland cried.
'With you are falsehood and evil pride.' "

"Is that you?" Lisa cries, looking across at Roland
in amazement.

"I'm afraid not; only I like to pretend sometimes"—
Roland winks—"that I might have been that Roland
in some long past life."

"Perhaps you were," says Mary McCamley. "Ah,
perhaps you were!"

Much later, leaving the adults, the children make
their way to bed, the twins first, complaining, then
Tom and John and Karen. The moon has risen full,

and Karen looks longingly at the shore, silvered and quiet, and wishes she could walk along it, but something makes her go on to bed, leaving the night to the grownups. She glances at them through the barn door as she goes to wash; they are dark shapes against the moonlit water. Their voices murmur contentedly, pipe smoke drifts on the breeze, and Mary McCamley laughs softly. Somewhere a night bird cries.

Karen gets into bed, propping the pillows behind her. There is a light on a cord beside her, and she takes up her notebook from the orange crate, where she has put a pot of mustard flowers and some shells from the sea. She feels snug and content, and in her mind words are going around. "The Song of Roland" speaks to her, the night and the sea sing outside her window, and she begins to think in words, in words of her own. Finally she leans forward and begins to write.

It is not connected writing, just impressions. Words about the sea, the shore, small bright impressions that run through her head. She writes until she is too tired to think, and then she lays the pad beside her on the table, turns out the light, and snuggles down. She thinks of Kippy, but somehow, lately, she has begun to feel that he is all right, that he is as safe and warm as she. She closes her eyes and she is fast asleep.

CHAPTER

16

The grownups have left the table and are walking along the shore, Bo tagging behind and Abbey left to peer after them from the willow tree.

"This," says Mary McCamley, "has been the most unlikely day of my life."

"How?" asks Jack Tillman, looking down at her.

Mary smiles. "Oh, the remodeled barn, and J.L.," she says, "and, I don't know, the kids in the village talking about Sand Ponies, the sheriff's office, eating lilies under a willow tree. And Roland and Sarah Paddyfoot." (These two are far behind, peering into tide pools.) "Having, suddenly, a room with a bed of hay and orange crates for a desk. I think I'm dreaming it all."

"Straw," he corrects her. "Straw, not hay. Well," he continues, "the way I look at it, nothing's nicer

than a dream. Right kind of dream, that is. I imagine
you'll find more things that are unreal, if you stay
here. It's different, somehow. Sometimes you think
you must have dreamed it. Or wished it." He glances
at her.

"Wished on the Sand Ponies, perhaps?" she says.
"Perhaps."

"I would like to see them, and make my wish."

"Perhaps you will, Mary McCamley. If you stay
long enough, I will take you to see them."

"When?"

"When you're ready to wish, of course."

Much later, when they have returned and Sarah
Paddyfoot has made coffee, Mary McCamley thinks
again of the ponies. "Haven't they ever been tamed?"
she asks.

"Not that I know of," says Jack Tillman.

"There's one in a corral, not far from here," says
Roland. "Don't know if he's broke, though. But fat,
looked cared for."

"Where is that?" asks Jack Tillman, and when
Roland tells him, he looks thoughtful. "You came by
the main road, then?" he asks.

THE SAND PONIES

"Yes, I did. Took my time—like to see the country. No sense in walking if you don't enjoy what you're looking at."

"What else did you see?" asks Jack Tillman, leaning back and lighting his pipe.

"Passel of things," says Roland. "Other wanderers. People. Saw some Sand Ponies once, loose ones. Passel of things."

"Ever see anything that made you wonder? That you didn't understand?"

"Most things on this earth make a man wonder, make him want to know more than he does, more than he can understand, maybe."

Jack Tillman is quiet. Mighty strange talker, for a tramp, he is thinking.

Sarah Paddyfoot is thinking the same thing. Mighty smooth answer, she thinks.

Ah, well, the night is growing cool, the moon is settling a bit, the sea laps peacefully, and the world is spinning so smoothly that a person cannot help but yawn and feel a bit snug, a bit happy, as if everything in the universe is in its proper place.

When Mary McCamley crawls into bed, between her own blankets, Abbey comes to settle down beside her. They snuggle close, for the night has grown cold.

Hmm, thinks Mary McCamley. Magic ponies, too. I think I've dreamed it all, I think I've dreamed this day. But still, I seem to be awake, and the straw *is* a bit stickery. That wouldn't be in a dream, now would it?

I wonder. Those Sand Ponies, I wonder if one could be tamed, could be broke. It has been a long time since I rode a horse. Why, I was younger than Karen. I want to see them. I want to see the wild little things, wish or not; there is something magic about anything wild, I guess. Something all of us yearn for.

She closes her eyes, and soon she is asleep, and through her dreams Sand Ponies run, rising from the dunes like fairy ghosts and streaking away before her.

The twins dream of Shakespeare, who has gotten strangely mixed with Roland into a symphony of screaming witches, white beards, pale dying ladies, bloody swords, and charging horses. Wonderful mysteries, here, to be unlocked. And with a real live teacher in the house, oh, what joys lie ahead!

CHAPTER

17

Dan Elber stretches his legs out and leans back in the sheriff's most comfortable chair. "It's them, all right, moving around up in the hills. Shouldn't be hard to catch. Whole bunch, except the mare. Afraid I've lost her. Her time's right due, may have holed up someplace, but it worries me. She was a nice little mare; gentle."

"Got some news for you," the sheriff says, getting his feet nicely settled on the desk. "Found your mare, too, Dan." Dan sits forward, eager. The sheriff continues, "Holed up in a draw near Lindley's Ranch; his boys found her. Got yourself a nice new filly, too. Born yesterday."

Dan Elber is grinning. "She all right?"

"Both of them are. Boys took them in, said the

mare was gentle as could be, glad to get some grain. Got 'em up at the ranch. Want to go have a look?"

"Sure do," says Dan Elber, getting up.

"It's her, all right," Dan Elber says as he opens the stall door. "Hello, Tolly, girl." The mare nickers softly. "Look pretty good, for going so far. Good keeper, you are, my girl. Well, can't move you for a while, now. Didn't like that snow much, did you, girl?" He is examining the colt. "Nice filly. Got us a nice new filly, sure," he says, rubbing the little ears. "Next thing is to get your buddies back," he tells the mare. "Fine bunch of no goods, taking you off like that. Suppose that buckskin pony had something to do with it. Smart aleck little thing. Well, won't be hard to catch 'em. Got room for a few strays someplace?" he asks the rancher.

"Sure, get my boys saddled up any time you say. Sheriff'll come, too, I expect, give us a hand. Plenty of room, plenty of feed, till you can move 'em. Wouldn't mind buying that mare, though. Nice little thing. Nice filly, too."

"Well," says Dan Elber, "I don't know about that. Thought for a long time about moving out of that high country. Gets pretty lonely, winters. But I don't know, hadn't thought about selling the mare. If she's gonna run off every spring, though, maybe I ought. We'll see. More inclined to find me a little place

around here, nice winters, and raise a few colts. Re-
tire, sort of. We'll see."

Saddled and mounted, the men start out from the
ranch. It is a long way up the draw to the hills where
the horses were last seen, and late morning by the
time the men spread out to work the hills. Kippy
watches them, and backs farther into the brush, nipping at the others and bunching them. No sense in
running; stay here, good cover, be quiet, that's the
best thing.

In the hills not far away Charley jerks at the ropes
of a sprung trap, swearing. Every trap is sprung, the
grain gone. "Dirty little beggars, look here! Every last
one!"

Tip grins, turning away. He likes to see Charley
foiled in anything. He is thinking, If Charley could
ride, he'd go after them horseback. I wonder why he
don't. Never have seen him *on* a horse; only trapping
them.

Setting new traps in new places, the men work
over the hills, Tip and Ed sullen, but doing as di-
rected, Charley growling at them when they are
slow. By the time all the traps are set in scattered
spots evening is coming on. They get back into the
truck and start for the ranch, Charley gruff and bad-
tempered. As they round a curve he slams on the
brakes and leaps out of the truck, for directly ahead

of them the Sand Ponies have started up, heading for the draw.

Grabbing a rope and looping it out, Charley starts down the draw on foot, running through the bracken like a moose. The men sit and watch him. "He's crazy," Tip says. Ed laughs.

Below, hidden by some wooded hills, the cowboys from the Lindley Ranch are slowly working toward the bracken-filled canyon where Kippy and his band are hidden. Kippy is growing uneasy. He twists an ear, listening. Something else is happening, off to his left. Suddenly, over the hill, a band of ponies comes running, straight for Kippy's hiding place. The cowboys are behind him; the ponies are coming on fast. Kippy leaps at the three horses, driving them out of the brush and down the draw as the ponies charge through the bracken nearly on top of them. The cowboys head for them, shouting, whirling ropes. It is nearly dark. The horses stumble, but down the ravine they go, hoofs pounding, a great swirling mass of them, Kippy in the middle.

The riders are on both sides of them now, trying to turn them; then one rider is in front, then another. Ropes whirl. Men shout. The band of horses breaks, spilling up the sides of the hills and down to the beach, running in the near dark. There are colts here, frightened, screaming. Kippy puts his head down and runs like a small fury toward the beach.

Then he is jerked up short, nearly falling. He

turns to fight the rope, which cuts into his neck. Ginger, too, is caught. The others have disappeared.

Rex is running in a tight little band that is headed for the beach, the pinto pony beside him, both stumbling as they hit the soft sand, then swerving away as two riders gain behind them, ropes ready.

Suddenly there is the roar of a truck on the road, the screech of tires, a crash, and then silence. The horses leap out onto the beach, jumping from the dunes down onto the wet hard sand and running along it until finally, pursued no more, they turn back into the hills, slowing to blow a little. All is quiet behind them.

On the road there are lights and loud voices. Riders are coming and someone on foot is running.

There is a groan from the wrecked truck, then another groan. Then there is a pistol shot; then a man's voice—"My God! Poor thing, truck ran right into her. What were you trying to do, mister?"

"He can't answer, he's too hurt," the sheriff says. Charley lies with his arm pinned painfully under the truck, unable to move. Ed and Tip have jumped from the truck and disappeared into the darkness.

"What happened?" asks Dan Elber, riding up.

"Hit a Sand Pony," says the sheriff. "Darn little critters. Really messed us up back there. Turned this truck over, too. I shot the pony."

"Sure it was a Sand Pony?" Mr. Elber asks, coming into the light. "Yes, poor thing. Well, she's out of her pain. Look here, she had a colt. Wonder where it's got to. May be hurt. We'd better look."

Kippy and Ginger have been led slowly up the hills to the ranch. It is a long way, and Kippy is almost too tired to fight.

Rex and the pinto settle down, then slowly begin to work deeper into the hills with the Sand Ponies.

Mary McCamley has gone to walk on the beach. The sky is nearly black, the sun long gone, and the sea is wind-swept and mysterious. As the wind strengthens she finds a sheltered place between the dunes and sits with her back against a sandy hill still warm from the day. Tall grass rustles above her and a few late birds hunt along the shore.

The little hollow is still and quiet. Maybe, thinks Mary McCamley, if I am patient I will see the Sand Ponies come down to the shore.

The wind stirs the grass, and behind the faint rustle Mary McCamley imagines she hears horses running, faintly, almost not a sound at all, running along the beach. Sand Ponies, running on the beach, she thinks dreamily, running over the dunes. The sound grows louder. Suddenly she stirs, sits up. I've been dozing, she thinks. The noise is louder. It is a noise; it is horses running; closer, getting louder. She stands up to see, but it is too dark. Now the pounding is like thunder. Men are shouting. Can she run? But where? Into the sea? There is not time.

Then suddenly there is the sound of screeching brakes, a crash, and the pounding thunder is nearly on top of her. She crouches down into the hollow in the dunes, huddling there. The pounding is all around her; dark bodies break across the dunes above her, leaping to the beach. More bodies, leaping across the dunes; then they are past, running down the hard-packed sand along the edge of the water.

She can hear men's voices behind her. She waits. There is no more sound of horses; she gets up. She doesn't want to see what is behind her, she wants to get away from it. She starts down the beach toward home; then she stops. There is something on the beach ahead of her. Something no bigger than a dog. She goes closer.

It is a tiny colt, looking dazed, shaking and breathing very hard. She takes off her scarf to tie him, but then she thinks, He won't know how to lead. Can I carry him? She tries to pick him up. He is heavy, but she gets him settled, finally, legs dangling. He is too tired to resist her, his sides wet and his breath still coming in great gasps. She hurries as fast as she can, nearly falling when she reaches the barn.

"Bring him in, bring him in," says Sarah Paddyfoot, seeing Mary standing uncertainly in the door. "My heavens, child. What on earth have you got? Get some straw, John. Tom, fix a stall. Poor thing, poor little thing."

They get the colt into a stall, still standing, but

dazed. "Get a blanket, John, and wrap him up,"
Sarah says. "Hurry!" But John is already there with
one, folding it around the little creature.

"What's the matter with him?" Karen says. "Oh,
poor thing!"

"I think he's only tired and frightened," Tom says,
feeling the colt all over.

The twins have come to the doorway, pajamaed

and staring. "It's a fairy colt, a Sand Pony colt," Lisa whispers. Jana nods, eyes wide. "Where is his mother?"

"It's a little stud colt," says John, rubbing the tiny head with a towel. "Looks black, but he'll be gray, I'd guess."

"A little stallion," says Tom, "with one white foot. Whatever happened to him? How *did* he get off by himself?"

It is much later when Jack Tillman comes in with the sheriff and Mr. Elber. The colt is warmer and moving about, sucking canned milk from John's fingers. The twins are snug in one corner of the stall, covered with a blanket, and Mary sits in the straw near them, watching the colt.

"Why, here he is," says Dan Elber. "Here's the little one. Spent half the night looking for him. Let's see, boy. Why, he looks fine. Orphan," he says. "Mother hit on the road. No marks on him?" he asks Tom.

"No. He's all right, I think. But what happened?"

"First, better fix it so he can get some more milk in him," says Jack Tillman. "Get an old inner tube, John."

Soon the rubber inner tube is cut and folded into a makeshift nipple, and the colt is getting his dinner, Mary McCamley holding the bottle as he drinks.

"I've got a mare with a new colt. Might take this one, too," says Mr. Elber. "Don't know, but we can try. We'll take him up there in the morning and see what she makes of him."

"But he's yours, I reckon," says the sheriff, seeing Mary McCamley's face. "Finders, keepers, looks like. Sand Pony colt."

Mary smiles and hugs the colt.

"Told you! Told you it was a fairy colt," shouts Jana. "Sand Pony colt!"

"Shhh," says Mary, "you'll frighten him." She looks at Jack Tillman. "People say you can't tame them. Is that true?"

He smiles. "No, you have a young one there. He'll be tame as a kitten, if you care for him like that, Mary McCamley."

"Of course he will," says Dan Elber. "Can break him yourself, likely."

"Now," says Sarah Paddyfoot, bringing coffee and drawing up boxes to sit on, "I'm about to bust, wondering what's been going on. Last thing we knew, there was a noise like thunder, then something sounded like a wreck on the road and Mr. Tillman was out of here in a flash. Thought I heard a shot, too," she says. "Made the children stay here. What's been happening out there?"

Having gotten himself settled on a nail keg, coffee balanced on his knee, the sheriff leans back against the wall. "Dan here," he says, "had got himself some horses lost up in the hills. We were out after them, with the boys from Lindley's. We were working down into the draw, when all of a sudden that bunch of Sand Ponies came boiling down the hills, and the next thing, Dan's horses broke out right in front of us, the ponies on their tails, and it was getting so dark you could hardly see. All mixed up together, the whole bunch of 'em—couldn't tell what you were roping. Little varmints messed up the whole thing. There was someone chasing them, though. Man on foot. Must have been crazy, running down the draw swinging his rope. Finally got tired and went back to his truck.

"The horses kept on down to the beach. We got a couple roped, and the others split up, some coming on across the road. That's when the truck came barreling down. Crazy fool! A wonder he only hit one. Had to shoot her. Got the ambulance, finally, took the man away. Dan went hunting for the colt. Mr. Tillman, too. Gave up finally; came back here to get warm."

"You didn't catch all your horses, then?" Karen asks, looking at Mr. Elber.

"Oh, we'll get out in the morning, try to find them," he says. "Got three, two still loose. Shouldn't be any trouble, if those Sand Ponies stay out of it."

The colt has lain down finally, full of milk, and sleepy. Mary sits beside him, rubbing his ears.

Jack Tillman watches her. "You want your bed in here tonight?" he asks.

She looks up at him and nods.

"Can we, too?" shout the twins. "Can we?"

"No," says Mr. Tillman. "Scoot!" And he smacks the closest bottom, sending J.L. off to bed, complaining.

When they have tucked themselves in, Jana says, "We'll go back when everyone is asleep. Miss McCamley won't mind."

"Are you sure?"

"I said so!"

But by the time everyone is asleep, so are the twins. Mary McCamley crawls into her bed and reaches out her hand to feel the colt's soft neck. Abbey snuggles next to her, purring, not minding the colt at all.

CHAPTER

18

Mary wakes to find a warm muzzle in her face, and sits up to stare into gentle colt eyes. She puts on her robe and heads for the kitchen to heat some milk, but Sarah Paddyfoot is there before her, holding the bottle out.

She's pretty in the morning, too, thinks Sarah. Well, what's for breakfast, now? Bisquits. Bisquits and blackberry jam.

When the truck arrives from the ranch the men tie the colt inside and Karen and the boys ride with him to hold him. J.L., mutinous, are made to sit in front.

The colt is unloaded trembling from his ride, but Mr. Elber soon has him calm again, then picks him up and carries him across the yard to the stall while everyone stands back and waits. "You must be still,"

Jack Tillman tells the twins. "Very still. We don't know what the mare will do, but if you upset her, she sure won't take that little one."

"Yes, sir," they say, subdued. They are as quiet as mice.

Mr. Elber goes in and shuts the door behind him. There is not a sound. They wait a long time, crowded into the tackroom, whispering.

Finally Mr. Elber steps out, closing the door, then stands looking into the stall. "It's all right," whispers Karen, watching him, "but he's waiting to make sure."

After an eternity Dan Elber turns and comes across the stable yard to the tackroom. "That's a good mare," he says quietly. "Took that little colt just as if it were her own. Not many mares would do that, not many at all. Good little mare, my Tolly."

Tom stares at him. "What did you say?"

Karen sits quite still, one hand raised.

"I said, why, I said that's a good mare, there—she . . ."

Karen interrupts him, breathless. "Her name. What is her name?" She is standing now, her hand on Tom's arm.

"Tolly," he says, looking perplexed.

Tom has taken off like a streak for the barn, slowing down only as he gets close. Karen is behind him. Mr. Tillman has reached to stop them, but is held back by Dan Elber.

Karen stands silently beside Tom, looking into the

stall. Tolly, nosing the new colt, looks up to nicker softly. Quietly, Tom lifts the latch and goes in.

Karen turns back to the tackroom, half afraid. Mr. Elber has stepped out to meet her. He takes her hand

and leads her around the barn to the corral in back. She stops still, then breaks away from him, running. Then she is through the fence and standing in the middle of the corral. Tears are running down her cheeks, she can hardly see for tears.

Kippy looks at her, ears up, then comes slowly forward. He pauses, looks puzzled, takes another step, and Karen's arms are around him.

CHAPTER

19

The sun is bright. A young girl sits astride a little buckskin horse, watching the pasture grass blow and the waves break silently far below them. Is this a dream? I am awake, Karen thinks, this time I am awake! Kippy tosses his head and wants to run. She smiles and pulls him up, scolding him.

She picks a path threading toward the sea, and down the summer hills they go, Kippy switching his tail and snorting. The air is bright and fresh, the birds call around them.

Overhead, breaking through the bird song, through the hum of crickets, comes a raucous cry. What is this in his field? The crow screams, circling, screams again, then goes on to see what else is out in his land this morning.

But only Karen is there, and Kippy, and the wild things which belong.

There are plans to make, questions to be answered, things to be decided. But not this morning. These things can wait; this morning is hers and Kippy's.

"Well," says Mary McCamley, pouring herself another cup of coffee, "what now, Sarah? What will Mr. Elber do? He won't take the children's horses home with him?"

"Not likely," says Sarah. "Didn't you see him, the way he looked?"

"Yes, but things have happened so fast! Sarah, I think it's all impossible, those horses coming all that way, and the children finding them. We're dreaming, Sarah. Must be!"

"Maybe it's the Sand Ponies," Sarah says. "Maybe they've bewitched us."

"I think they have. I do believe we'll wake up quite suddenly to find that none of this is real, perhaps not even ourselves."

"I feel real enough," says Sarah. "More likely just common magic, Sand Pony magic, made those horses and kids get together." Sarah grins. "Twins were right all along. Fairy ponies!"

"Hmmm, Sarah?"

"Yes?"

"What's to be done about Karen and Tom? School starts soon, and if they're not with their uncle . . ."

"Guess we'll have to help that wish a little," says Sarah Paddyfoot.

"I can send for their records, legally, but what am I to say they are doing here? Could Mr. Tillman be another uncle?"

"They'd check, likely."

"I'm afraid so."

"Need adopting, those two. Make someone a real nice family, they would."

"Mr. Tillman? But a man without a, well, a . . ."

"What are you stammering for?"

"What I mean is, the court wouldn't allow it, Sarah." She is blushing.

"Well," says Sarah Paddyfoot. "Yes, I see. It must be a proper married couple to adopt a child, not just a single man, I see."

"We can't let them be sent back, Sarah," Mary says. "Maybe we *could* lie about another uncle! And if we could fix it, then we must get Mr. Elber to sell them the horses. Do you think he will?"

"Kids have no money," says Sarah. "Maybe they could work it out, but . . ."

"Might do that," says a voice, and around the corner of the barn comes Dan Elber. "Way I look at it," he says, sitting down and glancing at the coffee pot— Sarah jumps up to pour, spilling Abbey to the ground, where she complains loudly and goes to Mary for comfort—"way I look at it," he continues, sipping appreciatively, "been in the mountains long enough.

Gets cold up there. Going to look around here for a little land, raise me some colts. Guess someone else has a prior claim to my best mare, but maybe we can work out a deal. Need some help, when I find a place.

"Way I see it, a boy can work for a horse he wants. So can a girl. Might even get me a wife one of these days, adopt those two kids."

"No need," says Roland, joining them from nowhere. "No need at all to do that. Taken quite a shine to those two—thinking just this morning of adopting them myself."

"You got a wife?" asks Dan. "Takes a wife, you know. Courts won't . . ."

"Thinking just this morning," says Roland, "of getting me a wife. Got just the one in mind; make a good mother for those two. Feed 'em lily bulbs."

Sarah's face is getting very pink. Mary McCamley turns away to hide her smile.

Sarah scurries toward the house, nearly running into Mr. Tillman and J.L., coming around the corner followed by the sheriff.

"Where is Tom?" says Jack Tillman. "Where's he gotten to?"

"Down the beach," says Mary, trying to look serious. "Down the beach with John."

The twins go running off, shouting.

Soon Tom is back, with John, twins dragging them.

"Sit down," says Mr. Tillman. "Get your breath.

Remember the deserted ranch, Tom? Remember Charley?"

"Of course I do."

"Well, it was Charley in that truck last night. Got him in the jailhouse. Got his friends, too. And some of the packages they were dividing up."

"What were they?"

"Money."

Tom looks perplexed. "Stolen money?"

"Counterfeit. You've earned yourself a reward, Son. Tell him, Roland."

"Well, that's about it," says Roland, settling himself at the table. "Been looking all over the country for that bunch. Thought a tramp might be able to move around without causing any concern. But by the time I found the place and had some evidence, you had reported it, Tom, and the sheriff had talked to my office and already had a man watching the Black Turtle when I got to town to see him. Reward's yours, Son. Talked to my boss two days ago. Drew a draft right away." He leans over and hands Tom an envelope. "Guess you could say the Sand Ponies caught Charley. One of them did, poor thing."

Tom looks at the check, then hands it back. "I can't take a reward. I didn't do anything."

"Yes, you did. You knew something was wrong. Didn't know what, but saw to it the sheriff knew, too. It's yours, Tom. You're to keep it."

"Well I, well I don't know what to say. It doesn't seem right."

"It's right, all right," says Mr. Tillman. "You can settle up with Mr. Elber if you like and bring Kippy on down here. We'll fix a shed for him, and Tolly, when the colts are weaned, or before, maybe. You can decide about Ginger and Rex. Got a good home with Mr. Elber, if they'll stay put!"

"And now," says Roland, getting up, "if you'll excuse me. . . ."

"Just a minute, there," Dan says. Both men head for the kitchen, but Sarah Paddyfoot has slipped out the back door and is going across the dunes.

J.L., seeing what is happening, leap to follow the men, but are jerked back suddenly by their father and sent, with Bo, to gather some berries for supper. The sheriff rises. "Must be getting on," he mutters. "Work to do, ticker tape to check. You boys give me a hand—think I've got a bad tire, may have to pump it a bit."

Later, in the loft, Tom finds J.L., berry stained, leaning over the window sill, arms around each other, giggling. "What's going on?" he asks, coming up behind them.

"Shhh," says Jana, quiet for once. "Look!"

Tom leans over the sill, then turns around and marches the twins away from the window. "Bad as the crow, for spying!" he tells them.

"What's this?" asks John, coming up the stairs.

The twins grab him, dancing around him. "They're arguing," says Lisa. "Arguing over Sarah Paddyfoot!"

And sure enough, in the yard below, by the willow tree, Roland and Dan Elber stand toe to toe, speaking very harshly.

John grabs the twins, pulling them away. "Go look out the back window!" he says, dragging them along the loft, laughing.

But Tom is there before them, waving a hand to hush them. The twins swarm around him, peering out; then Jana gasps, giggles, and runs down the stairs, shouting loudly, "Papa's kissing Teacher!" And this is the end of privacy for everyone.

"Looks like somebody's going to adopt you," says John. "Only thing I can't figure out is, Who? Sarah Paddyfoot's holding out against both, but I bet Roland wins; then there's only to decide whether it will be Dad and Miss McCamley, or . . . well, it's all too complicated for me. Just think, Lisa, real live teacher all your own!" He picks her up and twirls her around. Tom is staring at him.

Suddenly John is quiet, looking at Tom. "You're thinking I should be, well . . ."

"Yes, I think I would. I don't know . . ."

"It's been a long time, Tom. And Mamma was sick a long time. I used to go to the hospital to see her every day. We talked a lot, then. She used to tell me how she would feel, knowing Dad might spend the rest of his life alone. It was hard to understand. I thought she was kind of, well, funny because she was sick. But I've thought about it, since. I think now I see what she meant."

The crow is screaming in the front yard, and Karen has ridden up and is looking with amazement at the scene before her. Kippy, reins loose, is sniffing noses with Bo, and at the table two quiet men sit, while Sarah Paddyfoot, standing before them, gives them a tirade that outmatches the crow's. Mr. Tillman and Mary stand in the doorway, laughing, and the twins have piled out beside them, wide-eyed.

"And that is all I have to say!" says Sarah Paddyfoot, seeing her audience and turning away, angry, to march into the kitchen.

"What did she say?" asks John, coming out with Tom.

"She said," says Mr. Tillman, "that if anyone is going to marry *her*, they'll have to court her first, with all the trimmings! That's what she said!" He pauses and looks down at Mary. "And what about you, Mary McCamley, does that go for you, too?"

"Not me," says Mary McCamley, smiling. "Doesn't take me long to make up my mind! That right, Abbey?"

Abbey looks at her and blinks.

A breeze stirs the willow branches, and from the roof the crow scolds. A lone puff of cloud casts its shadow on the shore where sandpipers run, and far out on the waves a seal plays. Kippy shakes his head and stamps his foot. The sun shines brightly down on the barn and the willow tree.

Late that night, as Karen and Tom walk on the beach, he takes her hand and smiles at her. "I guess wishes really do come true sometimes."

Karen looks at him. "Did you wish to be adopted, too?"

"Of course. But it's not the kind of wish you tell, you know."

"Of course." They grin at each other. Overhead a late gull wings home, and the children turn and head toward home, too, leaving the surf to sing in the darkness behind them. Away in the hills, peacefully grazing, the Sand Ponies stir a little, and some lift their heads for a moment to gaze at the sea.

About the author

SHIRLEY ROUSSEAU MURPHY was born in California, where her father trained hunters and jumpers. She spent most of her childhood riding over the hills and beaches, and it is from these memories that *The Sand Ponies* is drawn. Horses also figure prominently in Mrs. Murphy's first book for children—*White Ghost Summer*.

Shirley Rousseau Murphy attended the San Francisco Art Institute and is a professional painter and sculptor whose work has been shown in much of the United States. She has exhibited in several shows with her mother, California painter Helen Rousseau, including the first exhibit by North Americans at the Instituto Panameño de Arte in Panama. Mrs. Murphy and her husband now make their home in Portland, Oregon.

175